張翔 / 編著

想去哪就去哪！

用**3**句
英文去旅行

隨書附贈 MP3
隨聽老外怎麼說

用**3**句英文，就可以玩瘋全世界！

祕訣
1 說對關鍵旅遊3句

祕訣
2 認識旅途中的重點單字

祕訣
3 收錄多元實用例句

使用說明

教你用3句英文，想去哪就去哪

1 旅遊情境全都包

出國在外，遇到事情怎麼處理？別擔心！本書包含各大旅遊情境，幫助你解決各種疑難雜症，不管在什麼情況之下，都能順利與老外溝通。

2 3句就能走天下

針對不同的旅遊情境，列出一定會用到的 3 句話。先提示每句話的使用時機，再學「也能這樣說」的進階說法，還有「對方可能的回應」讓你預先進行對話演練，碰到別人回答一長串英文，也能即時反應！

3 跟著MP3練口說

邀請專業的美籍老師錄音，讓你學習道地的美式發音，隨口說出標準英文！

④ 旅途中也要會這些單字

列出每個旅遊情境底下，你一定要認識的單字。就算一個人出國在外，只要對照、看懂這些重點字，旅途就能順利不卡關。

⑤ 要會說、必聽懂的實用應急句

列出更多你在途中會用到的、會聽到的豐富例句，還特別設計「一問一答」的短對話，讓你瞬間擁有應答能力，不再只是丟出單句的句子，卻無法和對方順利對話。

　　很多人在出國旅遊之前，常常想像自己被異國美景包圍，無憂無慮地逛遍世界各地，但在現實當中，經常會不知道怎麼問問題、看到一堆英文而心生恐懼，或是因為聽不懂對方的回答而雞同鴨講；難得出國旅遊，卻得花許多腦力、時間在溝通上面，實在非常累人。為幫助讀者跳脫語言的束縛，本書特別針對每個情境設計三大部分：旅遊 3 句、旅途中要認識的單字、以及應急實用句，來幫助大家化解出國玩樂常常會遇到的難題。

　　本書有以下三大特色：1. **旅遊 3 句**——在每一情境，教你只用 3 句話，就能提出你的問題，還會提示每一句話的使用時機、補充同義說法，並收錄對方可能的回應，當下就算聽到別人的回應，也能及時反應；2. **收錄旅途中會用到的單字**——當看不懂或不知道怎麼說某一單字時，就可以對照這邊的關鍵單字，輕鬆就能獲取資訊；3. **補充實用的應急句**——每一單元都補充你還可以說的、有可能聽到的重點例句，另外，還特別設計「一問一答」的短對話，教你如何回答別人的問題，順利進行雙向溝通。

　　希望讀者們能夠藉由本書，只要會 3 句英文，想去哪裡就去哪！難得出國一趟，就放下「英文溝通」這塊大石頭、放心地玩遍各地吧。最後，就祝各位讀者旅途順利、愉快！

張翔

CONTENTS 目錄

Part 2 交通完全攻略
Best Ways To Travel Around

Part 3 玩瘋充實行程
Enjoying Your Trip

CONTENTS 目錄

Part 4 手提大包小包
Time To Go Shopping

CONTENTS 目錄

Part 7 解決突發狀況
Resolving Problems

Part 1

朝目的地出發

Heading To Your Destination

Time to go for a vacation!

等了好久，終於要去度假啦！

名 名詞　動 動詞　形 形容詞

副 副詞　介 介係詞　片 片語　縮 縮寫

Unit 01

Packing Up For Your Trip

準備出國度假去

一定用得到～
3句話搞定旅遊大小事

準備去
度假啦

I'm traveling to Japan next month.
我下個月要去日本旅行。

 也能這樣說：

I am going on a vacation to Japan next month.
我下個月要去日本旅行。

對方可能這樣回應

Bon voyage!/Have a nice trip!
一路順風！

是否需
要簽證

Do I need a visa?
我需要申請簽證嗎？

 也能這樣說：

Do I require a visa to go to France?
去法國需要申請簽證嗎？

對方可能這樣回應

You need to apply for the Schengen Visa in advance.
你必須要事先申請申根簽證。

別忘記 必備品

Don't forget a travel adapter.
不要忘了帶轉接插頭。

也能這樣說：

Remember to bring a travel adapter.
記得帶上轉接插頭。

對方可能這樣回應

I already put it in my backpack.
我已經放進背包裡了。

旅途中也要會的單字 002

訂機票囉

airfare 名 [`ɛrfɛr] 飛機票價	**airline** 名 [`ɛr͵laɪn] 航空公司	**airline/plane ticket** 片 機票
budget 名 [`bʌdʒɪt] 預算	**budget airline** 片 廉價航空	**carrier** 名 [`kærɪə] 運輸公司
e-ticket 名 [`i͵tɪkɪt] 電子機票	**low season** 片 淡季	**peak season** 片 旺季

旅遊必備

business visa 片 商務簽證	**camera** 名 [`kæmərə] 相機	**charger** 名 [`tʃɑrdʒə] 充電器
converter 名 [kən`vɝtə] 變壓器	**student visa** 片 學生簽證	**packing cube** 片 旅行衣物收納包
toiletry 名 [`tɔɪlɪtrɪ] 盥洗用品	**tourist/visitor visa** 片 觀光簽證	**travel adapter** 片 轉接插頭

003

A Do you have any plans for summer vacation?
你暑假有什麼計畫嗎？

B I'm doing some budget traveling to Japan.
我打算去日本來個小資旅行。

Do you prefer a long-range tour or a short-range tour?
你比較喜歡長途旅行還是短程旅行？

I plan to go on a long journey.
我打算來一趟長途旅行。

I prefer a one-stop tour rather than a multi-country tour.
我比較喜歡定點旅行，不喜歡一次跑很多國家。

I have always wanted to go backpacking through Europe.
我一直都想去歐洲背包旅行。

A How often do you go traveling?
你多久旅行一次？

B It depends. I usually travel abroad once or twice a year.
不一定，不過我每年通常會出國一到兩次。

The first step of planning your trip is to decide when and where you are going.
規劃旅行的第一步就是決定時間和地點。

It is best to start planning at least three months prior to leaving.
最好在出發的三個月前就開始規劃。

I often go to websites to browse travel information shared by experienced travelers.
我通常都會上網查旅遊達人分享的資訊。

If you reserve airline tickets and hotels early, they may be cheaper.
如果你提早訂機票和旅館，或許會比較便宜。

Where are you traveling to?
你要到哪旅行？

If you are going to Vietnam, you have to apply for a visa.
如果你要前往越南，就必須申請簽證。

You can apply for single-entry or multiple-entry visas.
你可以申請單次入境或是多次入境。

A What's your dream holiday destination?
你夢想的度假地點是哪裡？

B My dream destination is Paris.
我一直夢想著能夠探訪巴黎。

A Have you ever been to Switzerland?
你有去過瑞士嗎？

B I've never been there, but I am dying to visit Switzerland!
我沒去過瑞士，不過我超想去的！

Booking Airline Tickets

買了機票就出發

一定用得到～
3句話搞定旅遊大小事

購買機票時

A round-trip ticket, please.
我要一張來回機票。

 也能這樣說：

I'd like to book a ticket to Chicago, please.
我想要訂一張到芝加哥的機票。

May I have your full name and passport number, please?
麻煩給我您的全名和護照號碼。

問特定班機

Do you have any flights in the morning?
有早上的班機嗎？

 也能這樣說：

I prefer a morning flight. Are there any seats available?
我比較喜歡早上的班機，請問還有位子嗎？

A moment, please. Let me check the timetable for you first.
請稍等，我先幫您確認一下班機時間。

When will it arrive?
哪個時候會抵達目的地？

🔊 也能這樣說：

What is the estimated time of arrival?
班機預計幾點到達目的地？

It will arrive at Dubai International Airport at about six the next evening.
隔天下午大約六點會抵達杜拜國際機場。

旅途中也要會的單字 005

班機資訊

business class
片 商務艙

code share
片（航空）共享班號

domestic flight
片 國內航班

economy class
片 經濟艙

first class
片 頭等艙

flight number
片 航班號碼

international flight
片 國際航班

one-way ticket
片 單程票

round-trip ticket
片 來回票

航線資訊

airway 名
[`ɛr͵we] 航線

direct flight
片 直飛航班

intermediate stop
片 中繼站

layover 名
[`le͵ovɚ] 中途短暫停留

long-haul flight
片 長途航班

non-stop flight
片 直達航班（班號不變、中間不停留的班機）

red-eye flight
片 紅眼班機（深夜出發、抵達時間為清晨的班機）

short-haul flight
片 短程航班

stopover 名
[`stɑp͵ovɚ] 中途停留

還有這些說法～
應急旅遊句會聽也會說

Have you reserved a seat?
你預定好機位了嗎？

It's a night flight, and the departure time is 11:15 p.m.
有一班晚上的飛機，晚上十一點十五分起飛。

Is it a direct flight?
這是直飛的班機嗎？

A **What's your destination?**
請問您的目的地是哪裡？

B **I plan to fly to London.**
我要去倫敦。

A **When will your departure date be?**
請問您出發的日期是？

B **I'd like to leave on the 15th of August.**
我八月十五日要出發。

A **How many direct flights are there to Boston every week?**
每週有多少班機直飛波士頓？

B **Three. The direct flights are on every Monday, Wednesday and Friday.**
有三班，星期一、三、五各有一班。

A **A one-way ticket or a round-trip ticket?**
請問要訂單程票還是來回票？

B **I would like a round-trip ticket, please.**
麻煩給我來回票，謝謝。

A When is your return date?
回程日期是？

B I am not sure. Can I buy an open return ticket?
不確定耶，我可以買不限回程時間的機票嗎？

There is a flight stopping at Singapore only for a short while.
有一班直達班機，只在新加坡稍停片刻。

The flight will depart from Hong Kong at 1 p.m.
這班飛機下午一點從香港起飛。

We've also got a morning flight, but you need to transfer in Bangkok.
另外有一班早上的班機，不過需要在曼谷轉機。

There are some seats available. Would you like to book now?
還有一些空位，請問您要現在訂機票嗎？

I am sorry, but the seats are completely booked at this moment.
很抱歉，目前機位全滿。

You have to pay the fare seven days before departure.
出發前七日須完成付款。

I can only afford an economy class ticket.
我只付得起經濟艙的機票。

Sir, your ticket has been booked.
先生，您的機票已訂位完成。

一定用得到～
3句話搞定旅遊大小事

確認預約資訊

I'd like to confirm my reservation to New York on June 1.
我想要確認一下六月一日往紐約的預訂。

 也能這樣說：

May I reconfirm my reservation to New York on June 1?
我可以確認一下六月一日往紐約的預訂嗎？

Your name and flight number, please?
請給我您的姓名以及班機號碼。

對方可能這樣回應

更改班機訂位

I'd like to change my reservation.
我想要更改預約的機票。

也能這樣說：

I'd like to change my flight due to some personal reasons.
由於一些個人因素，我想要改搭別的班機。

Which flight are you going to change to?
您想要改搭哪一班飛機呢？

對方可能這樣回應

臨櫃請求升等

Can I upgrade to business class?
我可以升等到商務艙嗎？

也能這樣說：

Is it possible to upgrade to business class?
我能夠升等到商務艙嗎？

 對方可能這樣回應

Yes, sir. You are qualified to upgrade.
沒問題，先生。您符合升等的資格。

旅途中也要會的單字 008

機票資訊

arrival date
片 到達日期

confirm 動
[kən`fɝm] 確認

departure date
片 起飛日期

gate 名
[get] 登機門

issue 動
[`ɪʃjʊ] 核發；發行

non-refundable 形
[ˌnɑnrɪ`fʌndəbl̩]
不能退款的

non-transferable 形
[ˌnɑntræns`fɝəbl̩]
不能轉讓的

personal information
片 個人資料

reconfirm 動
[ˌrikən`fɝm] 再確認

機場航廈

arrival 名
[ə`raɪvl̩] 入境；到達

business lounge
片 商務中心

concourse 名
[`kɑnkors] 大廳

departure 名
[dɪ`pɑrtʃə] 出境；出發

meeting room
片 會議室

prayer room
片 祈禱室

proceed 動
[prə`sid] 繼續進行

self-service 形
[`sɛlf`sɝvɪs] 自助的

terminal 名
[`tɝmənl̩] 航廈

009

Passengers should check in at least two hours before the scheduled departure time.
旅客在起飛前兩小時要到機場櫃檯報到。

I will check in three hours before departure.
我會在起飛前三個小時到機場報到。

A **Which terminal should I go to?**
我應該去哪個航廈？

B **Your plane will leave from terminal 2.**
您的飛機將從第二航廈起飛。

I almost missed the plane.
我差點錯過這班飛機。

A **What time does the next flight leave?**
下一班飛機幾點起飛？

B **If you miss this plane, there's another one leaving in an hour.**
如果您搭不上這班飛機，一個小時之後還有另一班飛機。

A **Will the mileage be credited to my account?**
這些里程有累積到我的帳號裡了嗎？

B **Yes, sir. You can also redeem credits within six months of your flight.**
有的，先生。您在六個月之內的里程都可以補登。

Your seats on Flight 694, departing at 10:30 p.m. on May 1, have been confirmed.
您於五月一日晚間十點半出發的班機，座位已經確認完成。

A I'd like to fly on May 15 on the same flight.
我想改成五月十五日的同一班次。

B Let me check your reservation. Your name, please?
我替您查一下訂位紀錄,請給我您的大名。

Your reservation for Flight TY-836 on February 26 from Chicago to Boston has been canceled.
您二月二十六日從芝加哥到波士頓的 **TY-836** 班機已完成取消。

A May I change to any flight two days later?
我可以改搭兩天後的班機嗎?

B I am afraid that all flights are fully booked on that day.
很抱歉,那天所有的班機都訂滿了。

A Do you want me to put you on the waiting list?
您想要排候補嗎?

B Please do so. When will you inform me if I've got a seat?
好,請幫我排候補。如果有座位的話,你們何時會通知我呢?

You sometimes can get an upgrade when you are traveling alone.
獨自搭乘飛機時,您有時會得到升等艙位的機會。

I have a business seat reserved, and I'm on standby for first class.
我訂了商務艙的位子,正在候補頭等艙的座位。

I think that I've earned enough mileage for an upgrade.
我覺得我累積的里程數足以升等了。

一定用得到～
3句話搞定旅遊大小事

找不到櫃檯時

Where is the EVA Airways check-in counter?
請問長榮航空的報到櫃台在哪裡？

🔊 也能這樣說：

Excuse me. Do you know where I can check in for the EVA Airways?
不好意思，你知道要去哪裡辦理長榮航空的報到手續嗎？

It's over there, next to Cathay Pacific's counter.
在那邊，國泰航空櫃檯的旁邊就是了。

對方可能這樣回應

辦理報到時

I'd like to check in.
我要辦理報到手續。

🔊 也能這樣說：

Hi, I'm checking in for the flight to Tokyo.
你好，我要辦理飛往東京的登機手續。

May I have your passport, please?
麻煩給我您的護照。

對方可能這樣回應

選擇好座位

Please give me a window seat.
請給我靠窗的位子。

也能這樣說：

I would like a window seat.
我想要坐靠窗的位子。

對方可能這樣回應

No problem. Your seat will be 34A.
沒有問題，您的座位是 34A。

旅途中也要會的單字 `011`

辦理登機

check-in counter 片 報到櫃檯	**departure board** 片 航班資訊板	**destination** 名 [ˌdɛstəˈneʃən] 目的地
first name 片 名字	**ground staff** 片 地勤人員	**kiosk** 名 [kɪˈask] 自助報到機器
last name 片 姓氏	**priority check-in** 片 優先報到	**surname** 名 [ˈsɜˌnem] 姓氏

選擇座位

adjacent 形 [əˈdʒesənt] 相鄰的	**aisle seat** 片 靠走道的座位	**legroom** 名 [ˈlɛɡˌrum] 腳能伸展的空間
middle seat 片 中間的座位	**next to** 片 在…旁邊	**row** 名 [ro]（一）列
seat 名 [sit] 座位	**specific** 形 [spɪˈsɪfɪk] 特定的	**window seat** 片 靠窗座位

A Do you have any seat preference?
您比較想要坐哪個位子呢？

B I am flying with my sister. We'd like two seats together.
我會與我妹妹同行，所以想要兩個在一起的座位。

A Could you get me an aisle seat?
可以給我靠走道的座位嗎？

B Of course. Just a second, please.
當然，請稍候。

Could I get a seat away from the lavatory?
我的位子可以離廁所遠一點嗎？

I don't want a middle seat, if possible.
如果可能的話，我不要夾在中間的位子。

Excuse me, sir. There are no seats at the front. How about seats in the middle?
先生，不好意思，前面沒有座位了，中間的位子可以嗎？

Let's head to the check-in counter. We're flying Singapore Airlines.
我們過去新加坡航空的櫃檯報到吧。

For international flights, you are obliged to present a passport as you check in.
若搭乘國際航班，在櫃檯報到時都必須出示護照。

The check-in doesn't start until another two hours.

兩個小時之後才開始辦理登機。

Here is your boarding pass and passport.
這是您的登機證和護照。

These are your baggage tags.
這些是您的行李貼條。

One goes on your suitcase and the other is for the baggage claim.
一張請貼在您的行李箱上，另一張是認領行李用的。

The flight will begin boarding around 8:15 a.m., at Gate A6.
班機將於上午八點十五分，在 A6 登機門開放登機。

When you check in with an e-ticket, you only have to show your passport to get your boarding pass.
若持電子機票報到，只需要出示護照就可以拿到登機證。

Do you require any special assistance?
您有任何特殊需求嗎？

A I don't see your reservation on our computer.
我在電腦上沒有看到您的訂位資訊。

B It's impossible. I made a reservation, and here is my ticket.
怎麼可能，我確實有訂位，機票在這裡。

Sir, I am afraid you are at the wrong counter. We are China Airlines, not EVA Airways.
先生，您走錯櫃檯了。這裡是華航的櫃檯，不是長榮的櫃檯。

Checking In Bags & Going Through Security Inspection

託運行李與過安檢

一定用得到～
3句話搞定旅遊大小事

詢問行李數量

How many bags can I check in?
我可以託運幾件行李？

 —也能這樣說：

How many pieces of baggage can I take?
我可以帶幾件行李？

> **Each person is allowed to carry two pieces of baggage.**
> 每位旅客可以攜帶兩件行李。

對方可能這樣回應

詢問行李限重

What is the free baggage allowance?
免費的行李限重是多少？

 —也能這樣說：

What is my allowance for checked baggage?
我可以帶多少公斤的行李？

> **Each passenger is allowed a total of 20 kilos on economy, 30 kilos on business, and 40 kilos on first class.**
> 每位經濟艙的旅客可攜帶二十公斤的行李，商務艙三十公斤，頭等艙則為四十公斤。

對方可能這樣回應

可否攜帶某物

Can I bring lotion on board?
我可以帶乳液上機嗎？

也能這樣說：

Am I allowed to bring my lotion in my carry-on?
我的隨身行李可以帶乳液嗎？

 對方可能這樣回應

Those items are permitted if they are less than 3.4 ounces.
每樣少於一百毫升的話，才能帶上機。

旅途中也要會的單字 014

 行李須知

baggage 名
[`bægɪdʒ]（美）行李

baggage allowance 片
行李限額

carry-on/hand baggage 片
隨身行李

checked baggage 片
託運的行李

excess baggage 片
超重的行李

luggage 名
[`lʌgɪdʒ]（英）行李

oversized 形
[`ovɚ,saɪzd] 過大的

overweight 形
[`ovɚ,wet] 過重的

weigh 動
[we] 秤重

 X 光掃描

container 名
[kən`tenɚ] 容器

forbid 動
[fɚ`bɪd] 禁止；不允許

inflammable 形
[ɪn`flæməbl̩] 易燃的

liquid 名
[`lɪkwɪd] 液體

permit 動
[pɚ`mɪt] 允許；准許

restriction 名
[rɪ`strɪkʃən] 限制

security checkpoint 片
安檢處

sharp 形
[ʃɑrp] 鋒利的；尖的

X-ray 名
[`ɛks`re] X 光

015

A How many bags will you be checking today?
您今天有幾件行李要託運呢？

B I'll check these two and carry my handbag on the plane.
我要託運這兩件行李，但我會把手提袋帶上機。

May I see your carry-on bag, please?
我可以看一下您的登機行李嗎？

Airlines have special restrictions on carry-on baggage.
針對隨身行李，航空公司通常都會有特別的規定。

A carry-on bag can weigh up to 7 kg.
一件登機行李限重七公斤。

Please put your check-in bags on the scale.
請將您的託運行李放到磅秤上面。

Is my luggage overweight?
我的行李有超重嗎？

I'm sorry, but you have to pay an excess baggage charge.
很抱歉，您必須支付行李超重的費用。

There will be an excess baggage fee of $600.
行李超重的費用總共為六百元。

Will the baggage be checked through to my

destination?
行李會直接託運到我的目的地嗎？

🔊 **Please check my luggage all the way through to Tokyo.**
麻煩將我的行李直接掛到東京。

🔊 **Let's proceed to the security checkpoint.**
我們去安檢區吧。

🔊 **Please empty out your pockets and put all metal objects in this tray.**
請你們把口袋中的東西拿出來，並將所有金屬物品放在盤子上。

🔊 **Please take off your shoes as well.**
請你也把鞋子脫掉。

🔊 **The metal detector beeped as I walked through.**
我通過檢測門時，金屬探測器就響了。

🔊 **Please step back, sir. Are you wearing any metal accessories?**
先生，請退後一步。您身上有任何金屬製品嗎？

🔊 **The metal buckle on your belt may have set it off.**
可能是您的皮帶扣環引起的。

🔊 **Please step through the detector again, sir.**
先生，請再走過金屬探測器一次。

🔊 **Step aside, please. We'll have to do a special check of your clothes.**
請靠邊站，我們得特別檢查您的衣物。

Unit 06

Ready For Boarding & Duty-Free Shopping

登機之前逛逛免稅店

一定用得到～
3句話搞定旅遊大小事

確認登機門

What is the gate number, again?
再請問一次，是幾號登機門呢？

🔊 也能這樣說：

Could you please repeat the gate number?
可以麻煩你再講一次登機門的號碼嗎？

> **You board at Gate A6. You can follow the signs.**
> 是 A6 號登機門，您可以跟著指標走。

對方可能這樣回應

確認登機時間

What time does the flight board?
這班飛機什麼時候開始登機呢？

🔊 也能這樣說：

When are we boarding?
我們什麼時候可以登機呢？

> **We'll begin boarding half an hour before the plane takes off.**
> 起飛前半個小時將會開放登機。

對方可能這樣回應

飛機誤點時

Is the plane on schedule?
飛機會準時起飛嗎？

 也能這樣說：

Is Japan Airlines Flight 509 departing on time?
日本航空的 509 班機會準時起飛嗎？

 對方可能這樣回應

I'm afraid that your flight will be delayed for 50 minutes.
您的班機恐怕會延遲五十分鐘。

旅途中也要會的單字 017

 登機時刻

board 動 [bord] 登機	**boarding pass** 片 登機證	**boarding time** 片 登機時間
delay 名動 [dɪˋle] 延遲	**departure lounge** 片 候機大廳	**on board** 片 在飛機 / 船 / 火車上
on time 片 準時	**passenger** 名 [ˋpæsn̩dʒɚ] 乘客	**runway** 名 [ˋrʌn͵we] 機場跑道

免稅商品

chocolate 名 [ˋtʃɑkəlɪt] 巧克力	**cosmetic** 名 [kɑzˋmɛtɪk] 化妝品	**duty** 名 [ˋdjutɪ] 關稅
duty-free 形 [ˋdjutɪˋfri] 免稅的	**jewelry** 名 [ˋdʒuəlrɪ] 珠寶	**liquor** 名 [ˋlɪkɚ] 酒
perfume 名 [pɚˋfjum] 香水	**purchase** 名動 [ˋpɝtʃəs] 購買	**tax** 名 [tæks] 稅金

還有這些說法～
應急旅遊句會聽也會說

📢 **Due to weather conditions, all flights to Japan will be delayed.**
由於天候因素，所有飛往日本的航班都將延後起飛。

📢 **Our flight was delayed for three hours due to some engine problems.**
我們的班機因為引擎故障而誤點了三個小時。

📢 **We will inform all passengers of the updated departure times ASAP.**
我們將盡快通知各位旅客新的起飛時間。

📢 **The details will be shown on the flight information board.**
詳細資訊將顯示在班機訊息板上。

Ⓐ **It's still early. Do you want to buy anything?**
時間還很早，你想要買點東西嗎？

Ⓑ **I want to buy some perfume.**
我想要買一些香水。

📢 **What's my duty-free wine and cigarettes allowance?**
請問我帶免稅菸酒的限額是多少？

📢 **Only ticketed passengers can purchase duty-free items.**
只有持有機票的乘客才可以購買免稅商品。

📢 **We can't get on the plane until they make the boarding call.**

還沒廣播登機之前，我們無法登機。

Attention, please. The boarding gate for Flight TY-836 to Tokyo has changed to A10.
各位乘客請注意，TY-836 往東京的班機將改至 A10 登機門登機。

Passengers of Flight TY-836 please proceed to Gate A10 for boarding.
搭乘 TY-836 班機的旅客請前往 A10 登機門準備登機。

Please have your boarding pass handy.
請將您的登機證拿在手上。

We are boarding now. All passengers on Flight CX-463 should proceed to Gate A18 for boarding.
我們現在進行登機，所有搭乘 CX-463 的旅客請前往 A18 登機門準備登機。

We invite passengers with small children or those requiring special assistance to come to the boarding counter.
請有帶小孩以及需要特別幫助的旅客前往登機門準備登機。

All passengers seated in rows 56 to 70 may now board.
現在請座位在五十六排到七十排的乘客進行登機。

We will now be accepting all remaining passengers to board.
現在請其餘所有的旅客進行登機。

一定用得到～
3句話搞定旅遊大小事

019

詢問座位在哪

I couldn't find my seat. Where is 32C?
我找不到我的座位，請問 32C 在哪裡？

◁) 也能這樣說：

Can you tell me where seat 32C is?
可以告訴我座位 32C 在哪裡嗎？

對方可能這樣回應

This way, please.
這邊請。

別人坐錯位子

Excuse me. I am afraid you are in the wrong seat.
不好意思，你應該坐錯位子了。

◁) 也能這樣說：

I think this is my seat.
這應該是我的位子喔。

對方可能這樣回應

Oh, sorry. My fault. So...12B is a window seat?
抱歉，我坐錯位子了，所以 12B 是在窗戶旁邊囉？

Where is the lavatory?
請問廁所在哪裡？

也能這樣說：

Could you show me where the lavatory is?
可以請你告訴我廁所在哪裡嗎？

對方可能這樣回應

It is in the rear of the cabin on the right.
在機艙右側的後方。

旅途中也要會的單字　020

 安全講解

announcement 名 [ə`naʊnsmənt] 宣布；通知	**demonstration** 名 [ˌdɛmən`streʃən] 示範操作	**emergency evacuation slide** 片 緊急逃生滑梯
emergency exit 片 緊急逃生出口	**fasten** 動 [`fæsn̩] 繫緊；扣緊	**life jacket/vest** 片 救生衣
oxygen mask 片 氧氣面罩	**safety card** 片 安全手冊	**upright** 形 [`ʌpˌraɪt] 筆直的

 機上設備

altitude 名 [`æltəˌtjud] 高度	**call button** 片 服務鈴	**comfortable** 形 [`kʌmfətəbl̩] 舒服的
electronic device 片 電子設備	**lavatory** 名 [`lævəˌtorɪ] 廁所	**overhead bin/ compartment** 片 頭頂置物艙
reading light 片 閱讀燈	**seat belt** 片 安全帶	**turn off** 片 關機

021

🔊 **May I see your boarding pass? I can help you find your seat.**
我可以看一下您的登機證嗎？我可以幫您找到座位。

🔊 **There's someone sitting on my seat.**
有人坐在我的位子上面。

🔊 **Could we exchange seats?**
我們可以交換位子嗎？

🔊 **Could you put this bag in the overhead compartment for me?**
可以麻煩你幫我把袋子放到頭頂的置物櫃裡面嗎？

🔊 **The compartment seems to be full.**
置物櫃好像滿了。

🔊 **I'll put my purse under the seat in front of me.**
我把皮包放到前面的位子下面好了。

🔊 **Ladies and gentlemen, this is World Airlines Flight WL-006 bound for Seattle.**
各位貴賓您好，這是世界航空 WL-006 從台北飛往西雅圖的航班。

🔊 **This is head flight attendant, Ella Chen.**
我是座艙長，陳艾拉。

🔊 **On behalf of World Airlines, we welcome you aboard Flight WL-006 from Taipei to Seattle.**
謹代表世界航空歡迎您搭乘 WL-006 從台北飛往西雅圖的班機。

🔊 **The flying time today is about 11 hours and 40 minutes.**
預計飛行時間為十一小時四十分鐘。

🔊 **Our expected time of arrival is 4 p.m. local time, October 30.**
我們預計於當地時間十月三十日，下午四點鐘抵達目的地。

🔊 **Please fasten your seat belt.**
請繫好您的安全帶。

🅐 **May I use my laptop now?**
現在可以用筆電嗎？

🅑 **No, you may not use electronic devices until the seat belt sign has been turned off.**
不行，在安全指示燈熄滅之前，您不能使用任何電子產品。

🔊 **Sir, please keep your seat in the upright position.**
先生，麻煩您把椅背豎直。

🔊 **This is your captain speaking. We've reached cruising altitude, and I've turned off the seat belt sign.**
大家好，我是機長。我們已經到達巡航高度，且安全帶警示燈已經熄滅。

🔊 **Still, for your safety, please keep your seat belt fastened when you are in your seat.**
為了您的安全，在座位上還請繫好安全帶。

Unit 08 Asking A Flight Attendant For Help

詢問空服員

一定用得到～
3句話搞定旅遊大小事

022

索取物品

Can I get an extra blanket?
可以多給我一條毛毯嗎？

🔊 也能這樣說：

Could you please bring me an extra blanket?
可以麻煩你再給我一條毛毯嗎？

> **Sure. Just a moment, please.**
> 沒問題，請稍等一下。

對方可能這樣回應

特殊餐點要求

Have you prepared any food for vegetarians?
機上有提供素食餐點嗎？

🔊 也能這樣說：

I reserved a vegetarian meal when I checked in. Could you please check it for me?
我在機場報到時有預約素食餐。可以幫我確認一下嗎？

> **Yes, madam. It will be served soon.**
> 有的，女士。稍後就會為您送餐

對方可能這樣回應

急著上
廁所時
Is there another lavatory around?
哪裡還有廁所呢？

也能這樣說：

I can't wait. Are there any other lavatories around?
我真的很急，這裡還有其他廁所嗎？

There are more lavatories in the back.
後面還有廁所。

旅途中也要會的單字 023

機組人員

cabin 名
[`kæbɪn]（飛機）客艙

cabin crew
片 機組人員

captain 名
[`kæptɪn] 機長

cockpit 名
[`kɑk͵pɪt]
（飛機）駕駛員座艙

first officer
片 副機長

flight attendant
片 空服員

navigate 動
[`nævə͵ɡet] 駕駛；導航

steward 名
[`stjuwəd] 空少

stewardess 名
[`stjuwədɪs] 空姐

索取物品

blanket 名
[`blæŋkɪt] 毛毯

complimentary 形
[͵kɑmplə`mɛntərɪ]
贈送的

free of charge
片 免費的

headset 名
[`hɛd͵sɛt] 耳機

newspaper 名
[`njuz͵pepə] 報紙

pillow 名
[`pɪlo] 枕頭

refreshment 名
[rɪ`frɛʃmənt] 點心

slipper 名
[`slɪpə] 拖鞋

sock 名
[sɑk] 襪子（常用複數
socks）

If you need any assistance, please contact the flight attendant.
如果您需要協助，請聯絡空服員。

Could I get a toy for my daughter, please?
我可以要個玩具給我女兒嗎？

In a few minutes, we'll be serving soft drinks, followed by lunch.
我們稍後即將提供飲料和午餐。

A When do you start to serve dinner?
請問晚餐什麼時候開始供應？

B We're getting it ready now. It shouldn't be too long.
我們現在正在準備，不久後就會開始供應。

Ladies and gentlemen, we'll be serving dinner in a few minutes.
各位先生女士，稍後我們即將供應晚餐。

Today's dinner choices are fried noodles with beef and rice with chicken.
今天的晚餐有牛肉炒麵和雞肉飯。

You can see the menu in the seat pocket in front of you.
您可以看一下放在您前面座位口袋的菜單。

Do you have any instant noodles?
請問你們有泡麵嗎？

If you have any special dietary requirements, please let us know in advance.
如果您有特殊的餐點需求，請提前告知我們。

A Madam, we have fried noodles with beef and rice with chicken. Which one do you prefer?
女士，您想吃牛肉炒麵還是雞肉飯呢？

B I'd like rice with chicken, please.
請給我雞肉飯。

A Anything to drink?
您要喝點什麼嗎？

B Apple juice, please.
請給我蘋果汁。

A What kind of drinks do you have?
有什麼飲料呢？

B We have mineral water, juice, soda, beer, and wine.
我們有礦泉水、果汁、汽水、啤酒，還有葡萄酒。

A Are you finished?
請問您用完了嗎？

B Yes, please take away the tray.
是的，餐盤可以收走了。

All the lavatories are occupied.
洗手間目前都有人在使用。

The lavatories in the rear of the plane are vacant.
機艙後面的洗手間是空的。

In-Flight Entertainment & Other Assistance

機上娛樂和尋求幫助

一定用得到～
3句話搞定旅遊大小事

詢問機上娛樂

What entertainment can I enjoy on board?
機上娛樂有哪些呢？

 —也能這樣說：

What in-flight entertainment do you provide?
你們有提供哪些機上娛樂呢？

> **You can watch the latest films and TV shows for free.**
> 您可以免費觀看最新的電影和電視節目。

暈機的時候

Excuse me. I'm airsick.
不好意思，我暈機了。

 —也能這樣說：

I feel sick. Do you have an airsickness bag?
我不太舒服，你有嘔吐袋嗎？

> **Here is an airsickness bag. Do you need some medicine for airsickness as well?**
> 嘔吐袋在這裡。您需要暈機藥嗎？

身體不舒服時 **Do you have any medicine for stomach pain?**
請問有治胃痛的藥嗎？

也能這樣說：

Could you bring me some medicine for an upset stomach?
可以給我一些治胃痛的藥嗎？

對方可能這樣回應

Sure. Anything else?
好的，還需要其他東西嗎？

旅途中也要會的單字 026

機上娛樂

earplug 名 [`ɪr.plʌg] 耳塞	**in-flight entertainment** 片 機上娛樂	**in-flight magazine** 片 機上雜誌
laptop 名 [`læptɑp] 筆記型電腦	**monitor** 名 [`mɑnətɚ] 螢幕	**poker** 名 [`pokɚ] 撲克牌
remote control 片 遙控器	**tablet** 名 [`tæblɪt] 平板電腦	**video game** 片 電玩

行程顛簸

airsick 形 [`ɛr.sɪk] 暈機的	**bumpy** 形 [`bʌmpɪ] 顛簸的	**medicine for airsickness** 片 暈機藥
motion sickness 片 動暈症（暈機、暈車等）	**sickness bag** 片 嘔吐袋	**throw up** 片 嘔吐
thunder 動 [`θʌndɚ] 打雷	**turbulence** 名 [`tɝbjələns] 亂流	**vomit** 動 [`vɑmɪt] 嘔吐

還有這些說法～
應急旅遊句會聽也會說

🔊 **Duty-free sales will follow after the meal service.**
用餐後，我們會進行免稅商品的販售。

🔊 **Are you going to do any duty-free shopping?**
你打算買免稅商品嗎？

🔊 **Would you like a headphone for the movie and music?**
您需要一副耳機來看電影或聽音樂嗎？

🔊 **Shall I bring you a blanket?**
要幫您拿條毛毯嗎？

🔊 **Can you help me with this earphone? Something's wrong with it.**
你能幫我看看這個耳機嗎？它好像壞掉了。

🔊 **The headphones don't work. Can I get another pair?**
這副耳機壞了，可以再給我一副嗎？

🔊 **Can I ask you to lower your window blind, please?**
可以請您將遮陽板放下來嗎？

Ⓐ Why is the plane bouncing so much?
飛機為什麼顛簸得這麼厲害？

Ⓑ It's just a little turbulence.
只是有一陣亂流而已。

🔊 **We are now experiencing turbulence.**
我們現在正通過一段不穩定的氣流。

📢 **For your own safety, please return to your seat and fasten your seat belt.**
為了各位乘客的安全，請回到座位並繫緊安全帶。

📢 **Kindly remain seated until the "Fasten Seat Belt" sign has been turned off.**
請各位留在座位上，直到「安全帶燈號」熄滅後再開始走動。

📢 **It'll be fine as soon as the plane gets out of the turbulence.**
只要飛機脫離亂流，就沒事了。

📢 **I don't feel very well.**
我覺得不太舒服。

📢 **Do you have medicine for airsickness?**
你們有暈機藥嗎？

📢 **I'd better get the airsick bag ready.**
我最好先把嘔吐袋準備好。

📢 **The airsickness bag is in the seat pocket.**
嘔吐袋在座位的口袋裡。

Ⓐ **My ears are all blocked up./My ears are popping.**
我的耳朵感覺被什麼塞住了。

Ⓑ **Try chewing gum or try yawning or swallowing.**
試著嚼口香糖、打個哈欠，或吞個口水。

📢 **I still feel sick. Is there a doctor on board?**
我還是覺得不舒服，飛機上有醫生嗎？

Unit
10 Transferring To Another Flight
等待轉機和在機場過夜

一定用得到～
3句話搞定旅遊大小事

028

詢問轉機航廈

Where should I go to catch my connecting flight?
我要去哪裡轉機呢？

也能這樣說：

I'm catching a connecting flight to Taipei. Where do I go?
我要轉機去台北，要去哪裡搭機呢？

You can follow the signs to the transit hall.
你可以跟著指標去轉機大廳。

詢問候機處

Where shall I wait?
我要到哪裡候機呢？

也能這樣說：

Where should I wait for the connecting flight?
我要到哪裡等轉機呢？

You'll have to wait at the transit lounge.
你必須在過境大廳等。

機場貴賓室裡 **Do you have shower facilities in the lounge?**
貴賓休息室裡面有洗澡間嗎？

也能這樣說：

Are there shower facilities available in the lounge?
貴賓休息室裡面可以洗澡嗎？

Yes. You can take a shower, and then rest in one of our private rooms.
有的，您可以沖個澡再到單人房間裡小憩。

旅途中也要會的單字　029

等待轉機

airport hotel 片 機場旅館	**connecting flight** 片 轉機航班	**eyeshade** 名 [`aɪ͵ʃed] 眼罩
overnight 形 [`ovə`naɪt] 過夜的	**sleeping bag** 片 睡袋	**sleepover** 名 [`slip͵ovə] 過夜
transfer 動 [træns`fɝ] 轉乘；轉機	**transit hall** 片 轉機大廳	**wait for** 片 等待

貴賓獨享

access 動 [`æksɛs] 使用	**airport lounge** 片 機場貴賓室	**conducive** 形 [kən`djusɪv] 有助益的
shower 名 [`ʃauə] 淋浴；淋浴間	**smart casual** 片 正式休閒裝	**subject to payment** 片 需付款的
support 名 動 [sə`port] 支持；幫助	**ticketed** 形 [`tɪkɪtɪd] 持有機票的	**VIP** 縮 貴賓

還有這些說法～
應急旅遊句會聽也會說

🔊 **Is this the transit counter?**
這裡是過境櫃檯嗎？

🔊 **I'm transferring to Flight NH-6254 to Tokyo.**
我要轉搭 NH-6254 班機去東京。

🔊 **I'm a transit passenger for this flight.**
我是這班飛機的過境旅客。

🔊 **I am getting a connecting flight to Boston at the Seattle airport.**
我要在西雅圖轉機到波士頓。

🔊 **I'm worried about my connecting flight to New York.**
不知道我轉機到紐約的時候會不會順利。

A **May I stay on the plane?**
我可以留在飛機上嗎？

B **All passengers are required to disembark and wait in the airport.**
所有旅客都必須下機，並在機場候機。

🔊 **Do we have to pick up our check-in bags?**
我們要領託運行李嗎？

A **Can I leave my bags on the plane?**
我可以把行李留在飛機上嗎？

B **Please bring all of your bags with you.**
請帶著所有行李下機。

How long of a layover do we have?
我們中途會停留多久？

How long will we stop at this airport?
我們會在這個機場停留多久？

Guests can enjoy a variety of finger foods and instant noodles in the lounge.
旅客可以前往貴賓室，享用裡面提供的各式小點心與泡麵。

Lounges also provide beverages like coffee, tea, juice, beer, and other alcoholic beverages.
貴賓室提供的飲品還包括咖啡、茶、果汁、啤酒和其他酒精飲料。

The best thing is that you can take a shower there.
最棒的是，你還可以在裡面沖澡。

Most lounge staff at the desk can help you with your flight if you run into a problem.
如果對於班機有任何問題，櫃檯的工作人員都可以提供協助。

Some lounges also offer business services, showers or a specific zoned-off rest area for those in transit.
有些貴賓室還為過境旅客提供商務服務、淋浴間，以及專屬休息區。

This transit lounge offers passengers a spacious, yet cozy environment where you can unwind and wait in comfort for your next flight.
這間貴賓室提供寬敞舒適的環境，讓等待轉機的旅客可以放鬆身心，等待下一班航班。

Unit 11

Ready For Landing

即將抵達目的地

一定用得到～
3句話搞定旅遊大小事

031

詢問降
落時間 **What time will we arrive?**
我們什麼時候會抵達呢？

也能這樣說：

How much longer until we land?
離降落還有多久時間呢？

對方可能這樣回應

> **We'll be landing in two hours.**
> 我們將在兩小時後降落至目的地。

索取
入境卡 **May I have one more disembarkation card?**
我可以再要一張入境登記卡嗎？

也能這樣說：

Could you get me one more disembarkation card?
可以再給我一張入境登記卡嗎？

對方可能這樣回應

> **My colleague over there will bring it to you in a second.**
> 我的同事稍後將會拿過來給您。

What time is it in New York now?
紐約現在幾點？

 也能這樣說：

Could you tell me the current local time and date in New York?
可以跟我講一下紐約現在的時間和日期嗎？

The local time now is 9 a.m., November 8.
現在當地時間是十一月八日上午九點。

 旅途中也要會的單字 032

即將降落

approach 動 [ə`protʃ] 接近	jet lag 片 時差	land 動 [lænd] 降落
latitude 名 [`lætə͵tjud] 緯度	longitude 名 [`lɑndʒə`tjud] 經度	taxi in/out 片 滑行
taxiway 名 [`tæksɪ͵we] 飛機滑行道	touchdown 名 [`tʌtʃ͵daun] 降落	tray table 片 餐盤

下機之前

boarding bridge 片 空橋	disembark 動 [͵dɪsɪm`bɑrk] 下飛機	disembarkation card 片 入境登記表
fill in/out 片 填寫	immigration form 片 入境卡	instruction 名 [ɪn`strʌkʃən] 用法說明
local 形 [`lokl̩] 當地的	temperature 名 [`tɛmprətʃə] 溫度	visa exemption/ waiver 片 免簽

還有這些說法～
應急旅遊句會聽也會說

🔊 **Do you need a disembarkation card and a customs declaration form?**
請問您需要入境表和海關申報單嗎？

🔊 **Can you tell me how to fill out the arrival card?**
請教我怎麼填寫入境卡，好嗎？

🔊 **You can find instructions on the back.**
卡片背面有填寫說明。

🔊 **What's the actual flying time from here to Detroit?**
從這裡到底特律的實際飛行時間是多久？

🔊 **How long is the flying time?**
飛行時間是多久？

🅐 **What's the time difference between Taipei and Hanoi?**
台北和河內的時差是多少？

🅑 **Please set your watch back an hour.**
請把你的錶撥慢一小時。

🔊 **I'm afraid that I will have jet lag when I get there.**
我很擔心我到那邊會有時差。

🔊 **I'm still on Taipei time!**
我還在過台北的時間！

🔊 **We'll be landing soon.**
我們即將降落。

054

🔊 **Please make sure that your seatback is in the upright position.**
請確定您的椅背已經扶正。

🔊 **We are now approaching Incheon International Airport.**
我們即將抵達仁川國際機場。

🔊 **The local time is 3 p.m., and the ground temperature is 20 degrees Centigrade, 68 degrees Fahrenheit.**
當地時間為下午三點，地面溫度是攝氏二十度，華氏六十八度。

🔊 **Please use caution when opening the overhead bins, as heavy articles may have shifted around during the flight.**
打開頭頂的置物櫃時，請留意櫃中行李滑落。

🔊 **If you require deplaning assistance, please remain in your seat until all other passengers have deplaned.**
如果您下機需要幫助，請留在您的座位，先等其他乘客下機。

🔊 **Don't forget to take your personal belongings when leaving the aircraft.**
下機時請記得帶走您的隨身物品。

🔊 **Thank you for flying with us.**
謝謝您搭乘本次班機。

🔊 **We hope you enjoyed your flight and that we have the chance to serve you again.**
我們希望您滿意本次的飛行，並期待下次有機會再為您服務。

一定用得到～
3句話搞定旅遊大小事

034

問入境
管理處

Where is the immigration office?
請問入境管理處在哪裡？

也能這樣說：

Which way should I go for immigration?
我要在哪裡辦入境手續？

對方可能這樣回應

Please follow the sign and go to a
"Non-Citizen" window.
請跟著指標走，到「非本國人」窗口辦理入境。

被問來
訪目的

I am here on a vacation.
我是來度假的。

也能這樣說：

I am here for pleasure.
我是來旅遊的。

對方可能這樣回應

Can you show me your itinerary?
能否給我看一下您的行程表？

I'll stay here for a week.
我會停留一週。

也能這樣說：

I plan to stay for a week.
我預計停留一週。

Please show me your return ticket.
請出示您的回程機票。

旅途中也要會的單字 035

 證照查驗

expire 動 [ɪkˋspaɪr] 過期	**immigration counter** 片 出入境櫃檯	**itinerary** 名 [aɪˋtɪnə͵rɛrɪ] 行程表
passport 名 [ˋpæs͵port] 護照	**passport control** 片 護照檢查處	**purpose** 名 [ˋpɝpəs] 目的
renew 動 [rɪˋnju] 更新	**travel document** 片 旅行文件	**valid** 形 [ˋvælɪd] 有效的

 通過檢疫

body temperature 片 體溫	**contagious** 形 [kənˋtedʒəs] 接觸傳染性的	**disease** 名 [dɪˋziz] 疾病
fever 名 [ˋfivɚ] 發燒	**infectious** 形 [ɪnˋfɛkʃəs] 傳染性的	**isolate** 動 [ˋaɪsḷ͵et] 隔離；孤立
public health 片 公共衛生	**quarantine** 名 [ˋkrɔrən͵tin] 檢疫；隔離區	**vaccination** 名 [͵væksṇˋeʃən] 疫苗

036

All non-citizen travelers have to fill out an arrival card and hand it to the immigration officers.
所有非本國的旅客都須填寫入境卡，並交給移民官。

Would you show me your disembarkation card, please?
麻煩給我您的入境卡。

Could you get a Chinese speaker?
可以幫我找個會講中文的人來嗎？

Is this your first time in the U.S.?
這是您第一次來美國嗎？

A Have you ever been in the United States before?
您以前來過美國嗎？

B I've been here twice.
我有來過兩次。

It's my first time here.
我第一次來這邊。

I went to graduate school in the States three years ago.
我三年前在美國唸研究所。

A What is the purpose of your visit?
您來這裡做什麼？

B I'm taking an English course./I'm with a tourist group./I am here on business.

我是來上英文課的。 / 我是跟著旅行團來的。 / 我是來出差的。

A What line of business are you in?/What is your occupation?
您從事什麼行業呢？

B I am a high school teacher.
我是高中老師。

A How long do you intend to stay?/How long will you be staying?
您計畫要停留多久呢？

B I'll be here for three weeks.
我會待三個星期。

A Where will you be staying during your trip?
旅行期間會住在哪裡呢？

B I will be staying at a local hotel/with my aunt.
我會住在當地旅館。 / 我會住在我阿姨家裡。

A Where are you going to stay?
您會住在哪裡？

B I will stay in a school dormitory.
我會住在學校宿舍。

Do you have more than 10,000 U.S. dollars in cash with you?
你身上的現金有沒有超過一萬美元？

When did you get your last vaccination?
你最後一次打預防針是什麼時候？

一定用得到～
3句話搞定旅遊大小事

哪裡領行李
Where can I claim my checked bags?
我要到哪裡領託運行李？

 也能這樣說：

Where can I pick up my baggage?
我要到哪裡提領行李呢？

Just follow the "baggage claim" sign.
跟著「領取行李」的指示牌走就可以了。

對方可能這樣回應

行李遺失時
I'd like to report a lost bag.
我想要申報行李遺失。

 也能這樣說：

I think my luggage is lost.
我想我的行李遺失了。

Please fill out the form, and hand it to the woman there.
請填寫這張表格，再交給那位小姐就可以了。

對方可能這樣回應

無申報物品時

Nothing to declare.
我沒有要申報的東西。

也能這樣說：

I don't have anything to declare.
我沒有東西要申報。

對方可能這樣回應

OK. You may go.
好，您可以通關了。

旅途中也要會的單字 038

 領取行李

baggage claim 片 行李領取處	baggage claim ticket 片 行李條	carousel 名 [ˌkæruˋzɛl] 行李傳送帶
compensation 名 [ˌkɑmpənˋseʃən] 賠償	conveyor belt 片（行李）輸送帶	luggage cart 片 行李推車
luggage tag 片 行李吊牌	retrieve 動 [rɪˋtriv] 取回	tag 名 [tæg] 標籤

 海關申報

confiscate 動 [ˋkɑnfɪsˏket] 沒收	contraband 名 [ˋkɑntrəˏbænd] 違禁品	customs 名 [ˋkʌstəmz] 海關 （需為複數）
customs declaration form 片 海關申報表	declare 動 [dɪˋklɛr] 申報；宣布	examine 動 [ɪgˋzæmɪn] 檢查
form 名 [fɔrm] 表格	goods to declare 片 報關物品	regulation 名 [ˌrɛgjəˋleʃən] 規定

Where is the luggage from UA-752?
聯合航空 UA-752 的行李在哪裡？

Which carrousel is for Flight TY-836?
請問 TY-836 班機的行李在哪個轉盤？

Does the luggage come out here?
行李會從這裡出來嗎？

I need a hand with my luggage, please.
麻煩幫我搬一下行李，謝謝。

Excuse me. That's my luggage.
不好意思，你拿到我的行李了。

Where is the lost luggage counter?
行李遺失櫃檯在哪裡呢？

A **Excuse me, but my bag didn't come out.**
不好意思，我的行李還沒出來。

B **Show me your baggage claim ticket, and I'll try to find it for you.**
請給我看一下行李條，我會試著幫您找到行李。

The airline will pay you compensation if your luggage goes missing or gets damaged.
如果您的行李不見或是毀損，航空公司都會理賠。

Please deliver the baggage to my hotel as soon as you've located it.

找到行李後，麻煩盡快送到我的旅館。

📢 **Do you have anything to declare?**
你有沒有要申報的東西？

📢 **According to the law, you can only bring one carton of cigarettes.**
依規定，你只能帶一條菸入境。

📢 **Customs officers have the right to confiscate it if you don't pay the tax.**
如果你不付稅金，海關有權沒收物品。

Ⓐ **What's in your suitcase?**
您的行李箱裡面裝了什麼？

Ⓑ **Just some clothes and personal belongings.**
只有一些衣服和個人用品。

📢 **Please open your suitcase.**
請打開您的行李箱。

📢 **We'll have to get them examined.**
我們必須要檢驗一下這些東西。

📢 **You'll have to leave them with us for the moment.**
你得把這些東西留在這裡。

📢 **You may close your suitcase.**
您可以關上行李了。

📢 **Do you have any plants or meat products? Any fruits or vegetables?**
你們有帶植物、肉製品、水果或蔬菜嗎？

Part ②

交通完全攻略

Best Ways To Travel Around

Select the right means of transport for your trip!

慎選交通方式，讓你的旅途更加順遂！

名 名詞　動 動詞　形 形容詞

副 副詞　介 介係詞　片 片語　縮 縮寫

Unit

01 Asking For Directions

迷路怎麼辦

一定用得到～
3句話搞定旅遊大小事

尋找附
近地點

Is there a convenience store nearby?
請問這附近有便利商店嗎？

也能這樣說：

Could you show me the way to the nearest convenience store?
可以告訴我離這裡最近的便利商店在哪裡嗎？

Go down Al Street for two blocks, and you'll see one on your right.
順著艾爾街走兩個街區，它會在你的右邊。

對方可能這樣回應

詢問怎
麼到達

How can I get to Union Square?
要怎麼去聯合廣場呢？

也能這樣說：

Excuse me. Can you tell me how to get to Union Square?
請問一下，去聯合廣場要怎麼走？

You'd better take a bus. Going on foot will take you over an hour.
你最好搭公車去，要不然走路的話要走超過一個小時。

對方可能這樣回應

哪裡可以小憩

I am looking for a café.
我想找咖啡廳。

也能這樣說：

Is there any place I can get a cup of coffee?
附近有沒有地方可以喝杯咖啡？

對方可能這樣回應

You can find one just around the corner.
轉角就有一家。

旅途中也要會的單字 041

路上所見

block 名 [blɑk] 街區	crossroad 名 [`krɔs,rod] 十字路口	direction 名 [dəˋrɛkʃən] 方向；方位
footbridge 名 [`fʊt,brɪdʒ] 行人天橋	junction 名 [`dʒʌŋkʃən] 交叉路口	sign post 片 招牌
traffic light 片 紅綠燈	underpass 名 [`ʌndə,pæs] 地下道	zebra crossing 片 斑馬線

辨認方向

across 介 [əˋkrɔs] 橫越；穿過	between 介 [bɪˋtwin] 在…之間	cross 動 [krɔs] 越過；渡過
go along 片 向前走	in front of 片 在…前面	next to 片 在…旁邊
on the corner 片 在街角	opposite 介 [`ɑpəzɪt] 在…對面	straight 副 [stret] 一直地；筆直地

A Excuse me. How can I get to the the Louvre?
請問一下，要怎麼去羅浮宮呢？

B You can take a bus. It's more convenient.
你可以搭公車去，會比較方便。

A Where are you trying to go?
你想要去哪裡？

B I want to go back to the Shangri-La Hotel.
我想要回香格里拉飯店。

A I'm trying to go to Union Station.
我想要去聯合車站。

B Oh, you are heading in the wrong direction.
噢，那你走錯方向了。

A Excuse me. Where is the train station?
不好意思，請問火車站怎麼走？

B Go down Oak Street for two blocks. You will see the train station on your left.
沿著橡樹街走兩個街區之後，火車站就在你的左手邊。

📣 Is it located kitty-corner from the McDonald's?
是在麥當勞的斜對角嗎？

A Could you give me directions?
你可以告訴我怎麼走嗎？

B Do you have the address? It would make it clearer for me.
你有地址嗎？這樣我才知道你要去哪裡。

🔊 It's only a three-minute drive.
開車三分鐘就到了。

Ⓐ Could you tell me where the British Library is?
你可以告訴我大英圖書館在哪裡嗎？

Ⓑ I am sorry. I am a tourist here.
不好意思，我只是個遊客。

🔊 Sorry, I am new here, too.
抱歉，我對這裡也不熟。

Ⓐ Excuse me, is this the way to Rockefeller Center?
抱歉，請問往洛克斐勒中心是走這邊嗎？

Ⓑ Yes, it is. Just go down 5th Avenue.
沒錯，沿著第五大道走就會看到。

Ⓐ How long does it take to walk to Westminster Abbey from here?
從這裡到西敏寺要走多久？

Ⓑ It's not far, only about a five-minute walk.
不會很遠，大概走個五分鐘就到了。

Ⓐ Where's the tourist information center?
請問遊客服務中心在哪裡？

Ⓑ Walk along Maine Street until you get to a large park and turn left. It's right next to a pet shop.
沿著緬因街走，看到大公園左轉，就在寵物店旁邊而已。

Ⓐ How can I get to city hall?
要怎麼去市政廳呢？

Ⓑ I am heading for city hall, too. I'll give you a ride if you'd like.
我正好也要去那裡，可以順便載你過去。

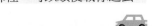

一定用得到～
3句話搞定旅遊大小事

043

哪裡可以攔車
Where can I catch a taxi?
到哪裡可以搭乘計程車呢？

🔊 也能這樣說：

Can I get a taxi nearby?
這附近攔得到計程車嗎？

對方可能這樣回應

The taxi stand is over there.
那邊有計程車招呼站。

請載我到某地
Please take me to Holiday Inn.
請載我到智選假日飯店。

🔊 也能這樣說：

Please drop me off at Holiday Inn.
請讓我在智選假日飯店下車。

對方可能這樣回應

OK. It'll be a 2-hour drive.
好的，車程大約兩個小時。

詢問費用

How much is the taxi fare?
費用怎麼算？

也能這樣說：

How much does it cost to go to the airport?
到機場要多少錢？

We charge according to the taximeter.
我們都是按錶收費。

對方可能這樣回答

 旅途中也要會的單字 044

計程車術語

cab 名 [kæb]（英）計程車	**cabbie/cabby** 名 [`kæbɪ]（英）計程車司機	**cabstand** 名 [`kæb͵stænd] （英）計程車招呼站
taxi 名 [`tæksɪ]（美）計程車	**taxi company** 片 計程車行	**taxi driver** 片（美）計程車司機
taximeter 名 [`tæksɪ͵mitɚ] 計程車錶	**taxi rank** 片（美）計程車招呼站	**initial charge** 片 起跳費用

與司機溝通

address 名 [ə`drɛs] 地址	**drop sb. off** 片 讓某人下車	**hail** 動 [hel] 打手勢叫住
hire 動 [haɪr] 使用；僱用	**hire a taxi** 片 叫計程車	**pick sb. up** 片 接某人上車
traffic jam 片 塞車	**trunk** 名 [trʌŋk] 後車廂	**limousine** 名 [`lɪmə͵zin] 豪華轎車

還有這些說法～
應急旅遊句會聽也會說

Will you call a taxi for me?
可以幫我叫一部計程車嗎？

The taxi will arrive in five minutes. The number is 558.
計程車五分鐘後會到，車牌號碼是 558。

You are not allowed to hail a taxi on this street.
你不能在這條街攔計程車。

A **Where are you going to, sir?**
先生，請問您要去哪裡？

B **The intersection of Loudon Road and Fifth Street.**
到勞登路跟第五街的路口。

Can you open the trunk for me, please?
可以幫我開後車廂嗎？

All taxis here charge according to the taximeter, so please don't worry.
別擔心，這裡的計程車都是按錶收費。

The initial charge is NT$70. Then, it's NT$5 for every additional 250 meters.
車費從七十元起跳，之後每兩百五十公尺加收五元。

How long will it take to get to the airport?
到機場要多久？

How long will it take? I'm in a hurry.

過去要多久？我有點趕。

🔊 **I can't drive too fast, or the police will give me a ticket.**
我不能開太快，否則警察會開罰單。

🔊 **Could you please slow down a bit?**
可以請你開慢一點嗎？

🔊 **Take it easy. You'll be there in time for your flight.**
放心吧，你一定趕得上飛機的。

🔊 **We can make it if there's no traffic jam.**
如果沒有塞車，我們就趕得上。

🔊 **Let me see if we can back out of here.**
讓我看看能不能從這裡倒車出去。

🔊 **Could you turn on the air conditioner, please?**
可以麻煩你開一下冷氣嗎？

🔊 **Could you open the window?**
可以請你開一下窗戶嗎？

🔊 **Just stop here. I'll walk there myself.**
停在這裡就可以了，我可以自己走過去。

🔊 **Could you stop somewhere here for a minute?**
可以在這附近停一下嗎？

🔊 **Just stop in front of the flower shop, please.**
請停在花店門口就好了。

一定用得到～
3句話搞定旅遊大小事

046

**購買
車票時**

Two single tickets to London Bridge, please.
我要兩張到倫敦橋站的單程票。

也能這樣說：

I'd like two single tickets to London Bridge, please.
麻煩給我兩張到倫敦橋的單程票。

對方可能這樣回答

That's ten pounds in total.
這樣總共十英鎊。

**詢問有
無座位**

Are there any seats available for Manchester?
到曼徹斯特的車還有座位嗎？

也能這樣說：

Is there any space on today's train to Manchester?
今天到曼徹斯特的火車還有座位嗎？

對方可能這樣回答

I'm sorry, but all seats are reserved.
很抱歉，所有的座位都沒了。

詢問車票價錢

How much is it?
這樣多少錢？

也能這樣說：

How much does it cost for a return to Pennsylvania?
到賓州的來回票是多少？

The cost would be \$117 for an off-peak return.
非高峰時間的來回票價為一百一十七元。

對方可能這樣回應

 旅途中也要會的單字 047

🗺 票券資訊

day pass 片 一日券	**fare** 名 [fɛr]（交通）票價	**get on/off** 片 上／下車
off-peak 形 [`ɔf pik] 非尖峰的	**peak** 形 [pik] 尖峰時刻的	**route** 名 [rut] 路線
ticket machine 片 自動售票機	**ticket office** 片 售票亭	**timetable** 名 [`taɪm͵tebḷ] 時刻表

🗺 交通工具

metro 名 [`mɛtro] 捷運；地下鐵	**motorbike** 名 [`motɚ͵baɪk] 【口】摩托車	**rickshaw** 名 [`rɪkʃɔ] 人力車
shuttle 名 [`ʃʌtḷ] 接駁車	**subway** 名 [`sʌb͵we]（美）地下鐵	**tourist bus** 片 觀光巴士
train 名 [tren] 火車	**tram** 名 [træm] 電車	**tube** 名 [tjub]（英）地下鐵

還有這些說法～
應急旅遊句會聽也會說

048

🔊 **May I have a timetable?**
可以給我一張時刻表嗎？

🔊 **Where is the ticket office?**
售票亭在哪裡？

🔊 **Where are the ticket machines?**
自動售票機在哪裡？

Ⓐ **Can I get an all-day pass from the machine, too?**
一日券也可以用自動售票機買嗎？

Ⓑ **No. You need to go to the ticket window for that.**
不行，一日券只能到售票窗口購買。

Ⓐ **Is there a nonstop train to Concord?**
有沒有往康科特的直達車？

Ⓑ **Yes, there's one at 10 a.m., and another at 5 p.m.**
有的，早上十點和下午五點各有一班。

Ⓐ **Are there any trains going to Charleston today?**
今天有沒有開往查爾斯頓的火車？

Ⓑ **Yes. Do you want to catch an express or a local train?**
有的，您要搭特快車還是普通車呢？

🔊 **When would you like to travel?**
你要搭車的日期及時間是？

🔊 **I would like three tickets to Manchester, please, for the 5 p.m. train.**

我要買三張下午五點開往曼徹斯特的車票。

🔊 **When will you be coming back?**
您回程的時間是什麼時候呢？

Ⓐ **I'd like a return to D.C., coming back on Sunday.**
我要買一張去華盛頓特區的來回票，週日回來。

Ⓑ **OK. Tickets for express trains are available.**
好的，特快車還有空位。

Ⓐ **I've booked a ticket for Boston online. Where can I collect it?**
我在網路上預訂了一張到波士頓的車票，要去哪裡取票呢？

Ⓑ **Please go to the ticket counter.**
請到售票櫃檯取票。

Ⓐ **Could we get a group rate?**
我們可以買團體票嗎？

Ⓑ **You won't get a group rate unless you have 10 in your party.**
要滿十個人才能購買團體票喔。

Ⓐ **Is there a student discount?**
有學生優惠嗎？

Ⓑ **Yes, it's 10% cheaper if you have your International Student Card.**
有的，只要您有國際學生證，票價就能打九折。

🔊 **Are there any reductions for off-peak travel?**
如果在離峰時間搭車，會比較便宜嗎？

🔊 **The children's fare is cheaper.**
孩童票比較便宜。

一定用得到～
3句話搞定旅遊大小事

詢問月台時

Which platform do I need for San Diego?
往聖地牙哥的列車要到第幾月台等呢？

也能這樣說：

Which platform does the train to San Diego leave from?
往聖地牙哥的列車會從幾號月台發車呢？

Let me check it first. You need to wait on platform 3A.
讓我查一下。您要到 3A 月台候車。

對方可能這樣回應

問末班車時間

When's the last train to New York?
最後一班到紐約的火車是幾點的呢？

也能這樣說：

When does the last train to New York depart?
最後一班到紐約的火車幾點開呢？

It departs at 8 p.m., so you'd better hurry up.
最後一班火車晚上八點開，所以你得快一點。

對方可能這樣回應

May I sit here?
我可以坐這裡嗎？

也能這樣說：

Excuse me. Is this seat taken?
不好意思，這個位子有人坐嗎？

I'm afraid this seat is taken.
這個位子有人坐了。

 旅途中也要會的單字 050

 月台候車

branch line 片（鐵路）支線	**feeder** 名 [`fidɚ] （鐵路、道路的）支線	**left-luggage office** 片 行李寄存處
on schedule 片 準時的	**platform** 名 [`plæt͵fɔrm] 月台	**platform ticket** 片 月台票
tunnel 名 [`tʌnḷ] 隧道	**underground** 名 [`ʌndɚ͵graund] （英）地下鐵	**waiting line** 片 候車線

 火車旅行

bed seat 片 臥鋪	**conductor** 名 [kən`dʌktɚ] 列車服務員	**dining car** 片 餐車
express 名 [ɪk`sprɛs] 快車	**locomotive** 名 [͵lokə`motɪv] 火車頭	**lost property** 片 遺失物
railway 名 [`rel͵we] 鐵路	**sightseeing train** 片 觀光列車	**waiting room** 片 候車室

還有這些說法～
應急旅遊句會聽也會說

A Where can I get a subway map?
地鐵路線圖可以去哪裡拿呢？

B You can get a free map at the information center.
服務中心有免費的地圖可以拿。

A I don't have any change. Where can I get some change?
我沒有零錢，哪裡可以換零錢呢？

B There's a change machine next to the ticket machine.
售票機旁邊有一台兌幣機。

📢 Does this subway stop at Rockefeller Center?
這班地鐵有停洛克斐勒中心站嗎？

A How many stops before Central Park?
到中央公園會經過幾站？

B It's just three stops away from here.
離這一站只有三站而已。

📢 Is this the right platform for Atlanta?
到亞特蘭大的車是在這個月台等嗎？

A When is the next train to New York?
下一班往紐約的火車幾點開呢？

B The next train will arrive in three minutes.
下一班車會在三分鐘後到站。

📢 Is this the train to Los Angeles?
這是往洛杉磯的火車嗎？

A Will the train arrive on time?
車子會準時抵達嗎？

B The train for Seattle is delayed.
開往西雅圖的列車誤點了。

The train will be arriving in ten minutes.
火車再過十分鐘就會到了。

Hurry up! The train is leaving soon!
快一點！火車快開了！

It will arrive in a few minutes. Let's get our bags from the rack.
再過一下就到了，我們把行李拿下來吧。

A You missed your stop, sir.
先生，你坐過站了。

B Gosh! I fell asleep and missed my station.
天啊！我睡過頭了。

I am afraid that you've got on the wrong line.
我想你可能搭錯線了。

A May I see your ticket, please?
可以給我看一下您的車票嗎？

B I lost the ticket. What should I do?
我的票弄丟了，怎麼辦？

What time are we expecting to arrive at San Francisco?
我們預計幾點會到舊金山？

Unit 05 Taking A Bus

一定用得到～
3句話搞定旅遊大小事

052

問站牌在哪裡

Where's the nearest bus stop?
最近的公車站牌在哪裡？

 也能這樣說：

Do you know where the nearest bus stop is?
你知道離這裡最近的公車站牌在哪裡嗎？

> **It's pretty near. Just go straight, and it's down the street.**
> 還滿近的，直走到底就是了。

對方可能這樣回應

問有無停某站

Does this bus stop at London Bridge?
這班公車在倫敦橋會停靠嗎？

 也能這樣說：

Do you stop anywhere near London Bridge?
會停倫敦橋附近嗎？

> **Yes. It's the first stop on High Street.**
> 有的，大街第一站就是了。

對方可能這樣回應

請司機提醒你

Could you tell me when we get to the Lincoln Memorial?
到林肯紀念堂的時候可以叫我一下嗎？

也能這樣說：

Please tell me when we get to the Lincoln Memorial.
到林肯紀念堂時請跟我說一聲。

對方可能這樣回應

Sure. I'll tell you when.
沒問題，到的時候會告訴你的。

 旅途中也要會的單字　053

搭乘公車

bus driver 片 公車司機	**catch** 動 [kætʃ] 搭上（車）	**coach** 名 [kotʃ] 長途巴士
double-decker bus 片 （英）雙層巴士	**line** 名 [laɪn]（美）隊伍	**night bus** 片 夜車
priority seat 片 博愛座	**queue** 名 [kju]（英）隊伍	**terminus** 名 [`tɜmənəs] 終點站

 公車上面

accessible 形 [æk`sɛsəbḷ] 易進入的（指有附設無障礙座位）	**bus fare** 片 公車票價	**bus lane** 片 公車道
bus station 片 公車轉運站	**bus stop** 片 公車站牌	**fare box** 片 車費箱
inspector 名 [ɪn`spɛktə] 剪票員	**request stop** 片 （公車）招呼站	**signal** 動 [`sɪgnḷ] 示意；打信號

054

🔊 Which bus should I take to get there?
我應該要搭哪一線的公車呢？

Ⓐ Is this bus bound for the zoo?
這輛公車是開往動物園的嗎？

Ⓑ No, this goes only as far as Children's Hospital.
沒有，這輛公車只到兒童醫院。

Ⓐ Could you tell me the bus number to downtown?
請問到市區的公車是幾號？

Ⓑ You should take bus No.36.
你應該搭三十六號公車。

Ⓐ Is this the shuttle into town?
這是進市區的接駁巴士嗎？

Ⓑ Yes, but this one is full. You need to wait for the next one.
是的，但現在客滿了，請等下一班車。

🔊 Do I need to transfer?
需要轉車嗎？

Ⓐ Where should I change buses?
我要到哪裡轉車？

Ⓑ You can change buses for the zoo at Park Station. Then take bus No.5.
你可以到公園站換車，然後搭五號公車到動物園。

🔊 Can you tell me where to get off for the Madame Tussauds New York?

到杜莎夫人蠟像館的時候可以跟我說一下嗎？

Please let me know when we get to the National Gallery of Art, OK?
到國家藝廊的時候可以叫我一下嗎？

A **How often does the bus run?**
這班公車多久來一班？
B **Every ten minutes on weekdays and every twenty minutes on weekends.**
週一到週五每十分鐘一班，週末每二十分鐘一班。

A **How much is the bus fare to the zoo?**
搭公車到動物園要多少錢？
B **It costs $6 for one way and $10 for a return ticket.**
單程票是六元，來回票是十元。

A **Should I buy a ticket?**
我需要買票嗎？
B **There's no need to buy a ticket. Just put the bus fare in the box on the bus.**
不用買票，只要把錢投到公車的收費箱內就好。

A **Where do I pay the fare?**
我要在哪裡付費？
B **On the bus. The conductor will collect the fare.**
車掌會在車上收費。

Excuse me. Is the next stop Freedom Square?
請問下一站是自由廣場嗎？

I'd like to get off at the next stop, please.
請讓我在下一站下車。

一定用得到～
3句話搞定旅遊大小事

I want to rent a car.
我想要租車。

也能這樣說：

I'd like to rent a car for five days.
我想要租五天的車。

> **May I see your international driving permit?**
> 可否讓我看一下您的國際駕照呢？

對方可能這樣回答

I'm here to pick up my car.
我是來取車的。

也能這樣說：

Hi, I'm picking up my car.
你好，我是來取車的。

> **Do you have a confirmation number?**
> 您有預約號碼嗎？

對方可能這樣回答

詢問車
上設備

Does it have air conditioning?
車上有冷氣嗎？

也能這樣說：

Has this car got air conditioning?
車上有配備冷氣嗎？

對方可能這樣回應

Yes, it has air conditioning.
有的，車內有裝設冷氣。

旅途中也要會的單字 056

 車型喜好

automobile 名 [`ɔtəmə,bɪl] 汽車	car rental 片 租車公司	convertible 名 [kən`vɝtəbl̩] 敞篷車
jeep 名 [dʒip] 吉普車	leaseholder 名 [`lis,holdɚ] 租賃人	rent 動 [rɛnt] 租
sedan 名 [sɪ`dæn] 小轎車	SUV 縮 休旅車	wagon 名 [`wægən] 旅行車

 租車須知

air bag 片 安全氣囊	dashcam 縮 行車紀錄器	driver's license 片 駕照
GPS 縮 衛星導航	instrument panel 片 儀錶板	international driving permit 片 國際駕照
mileage 名 [`maɪlɪdʒ] 里程	steering wheel 片 方向盤	windshield 名 [`wɪnd,ʃild] 擋風玻璃

還有這些說法～
應急旅遊句會聽也會說

057

A What kind of cars do you have?
你們有什麼樣的車？

B We have compacts, plus mid-size and full-size cars.
我們有小型車、中型車和大型車。

A How much is it if I rent a mid-size car for a week?
如果租中型車一星期要多少錢？

B The rental is $55 per day, and $350 for a week.
租金是一天五十五美元，一星期則是三百五十元。

A How much does it cost?
這台租金是多少？

B $40 a day with unlimited mileage.
一天四十美元，不限里程數。

📢 Does that include collision insurance?
價錢有包含碰撞險嗎？

A Do I have to pay a deposit?
我需要付押金嗎？

B You have to pay a deposit, but it is refundable if the car is not damaged.
您必須付押金，不過只要還車時車子沒有損壞，就會退還押金。

A Do you have any special deals this week?
這禮拜有什麼特別優惠嗎？

B Yes, we are now offering a weekly rate of $300 with unlimited miles.
有的，我們現在提供一星期三百元，而且不限里程數的優惠。

A What kind of insurance coverage would you like?
您要投保哪些項目呢？

B Full coverage, please.
我要保全險。

A Where are you picking up and returning the car?
請問您要在哪裡取車和還車？

B I'll pick it up at the airport and return it at your downtown branch.
我要在機場取車，再到市區的分店還車。

I need to take a copy of your driver's license.
我需要影印一下您的駕照。

You need to refill it before returning the car.
還車前請將油箱加滿。

A What's the charge if I don't return it with a full tank?
如果還車時沒有把油加滿的話，會加收多少錢？

B There is a two-dollar-per-gallon charge.
一加侖會收兩元。

A Can I return the car in San Diego?
我可以在聖地牙哥還車嗎？

B Sure, you can return it at any of our branches in California.
可以的，您可以在我們所有位於加州的分店還車。

You have to pay extra if you want to return it in another state.
若您想要在別州還車的話，就必須支付額外的費用。

一定用得到～
3句話搞定旅遊大小事

需要加油時

Fill it up with unleaded 95, please.
九五無鉛加滿，謝謝。

也能這樣說：

Tank up the unleaded 95, please.
九五無鉛加滿，謝謝。

對方可能這樣回應

No problem. Just a moment, please.
沒問題，請稍等一下。

車子壞掉了

The windshield wipers are not working.
雨刷怎麼不會動。

也能這樣說：

There's something wrong with the windshield wipers.
雨刷好像有問題。

對方可能這樣回應

Let's pull over and have a look.
我們先靠邊停車，檢查一下吧。

加油站服務 **Please wash my car, too.**
請順便幫我洗車。

也能這樣說：

Would you wash my car, please?
可以幫我洗個車嗎？

 對方可能這樣回應

Sure. We'll wash it right away.
好的，我們馬上幫您洗車。

 旅途中也要會的單字 059

車子組成

automatic transmission 片 自動排檔	brake 名 [brek] 煞車	engine 名 [`ɛndʒɪn] 引擎
gas pedal 片 油門	indicator 名 [`ɪndə͵ketə] 方向燈	low/high beam 片 近 / 遠光燈
manual shift 片 手動排檔	tail light 片 尾燈	windshield wiper 片 雨刷

路上遭遇

car wash 片 洗車	flat tire 片 爆胎	fuel 名 [`fjʊəl] 燃料
fuel/gas up 片 加油	gallon 名 [`gælən] 加侖	petrol 名 [`pɛtrəl]（英）汽油
petrol station 片（英）加油站	tollgate 名 [`tol͵get] 收費站	unleaded gasoline 片 無鉛汽油

060

📣 Fasten your seat belt! Let's hit the road.
繫好你的安全帶，我們出發吧！

📣 Where's the nearest petrol station?
最近的加油站在哪裡？

📣 We are running out of gas. I think we should get some gas first.
我們快沒油了，我覺得應該要先去加點油。

📣 Premium, unleaded, or diesel?
要加高級汽油、無鉛汽油還是柴油？

Ⓐ Does the gas station offer free car washes?
這個加油站有沒有免費洗車的服務？

Ⓑ I don't think so. But they offer other freebies, like toilet paper and bottled water.
應該沒有，不過他們有免費贈品，像是面紙和瓶裝水。

Ⓐ I can't get my car started.
我無法啟動車子。

Ⓑ You'd better check the water and gas.
你最好先檢查一下水箱和油箱。

📣 My car broke down on the freeway.
我的車在高速公路上拋錨了。

Ⓐ Can you hear a cracking noise under my engine?
你有聽到引擎發出的怪聲嗎？

Ⓑ You should pull over as soon as you can.

你應該盡快靠路邊停車。

🔊 I have a flat tire. Do you have a spare tire in your trunk?
我車子爆胎了，你的行李箱裡有備胎嗎？

🔊 Can I park here?
我可以停這裡嗎？

🔊 How far is it to the next service area?
到下一個休息站還有多遠？

🔊 Are we nearly there?
我們快到了嗎？

🔊 I was pulled over to the roadside by a policeman.
我被警察攔下來，停在路邊。

🔊 Don't drive too fast, or you will get a speeding ticket.
不要開太快，否則你會收到超速罰單。

🔊 Don't race through yellow lights.
不要搶黃燈！

🔊 Running red lights is very dangerous.
闖紅燈是很危險的。

🔊 Shift into the reverse gear and use the rearview mirror.
打 R 檔倒車，而且要透過後視鏡確認後方情況。

🔊 Obey the speed limit posted on signs along the roads.
要遵守路旁標示的最高速限。

一定用得到～
3句話搞定旅遊大小事

 詢問時間

Is there a morning ferry to Plymouth?
往普利茅斯的船早上有開嗎？

也能這樣說：

Could you tell me if there's a morning ferry from here to Plymouth?
早上有沒有從這裡到普利茅斯的渡輪呢？

Yes, it's eight o'clock on Mondays and Wednesdays.
有的，每週一和週三早上八點都有一班。

對方可能這樣回應

訂票這樣說

I'd like two tickets for foot passengers.
請給我兩張票。（foot passenger：沒有帶車上渡輪的乘客）

也能這樣說：

I'd like a ticket for a car and two passengers.
我要兩個人的票，還有一輛車要上船。

Sure. Do you need a cabin?
好的，您們需要艙房嗎？

對方可能這樣回應

詢問額外費用

What about taking my car, will that be extra?
如果帶上車子的話，要加費用嗎？

也能這樣說：

Does it cost extra if I take my car on board?
帶車子上船的話要多付錢嗎？

對方可能這樣回應

Yes, that'd be $40 each way.
要，單程是四十美金。

 旅途中也要會的單字 062

水上交通

boat 名 [bot] 船	cruise ship 片 郵輪	embark 動 [ɪmˋbɑrk] 上船 / 飛機
ferry 名 [ˋfɛrɪ] 渡輪	harbor 名 [ˋhɑrbɚ] 海港	port 名 [port] 港口
sail 動 [sel] 航行；開船	seasick 形 [ˋsi͵sɪk] 暈船的	yacht 名 [jɑt] 快艇；遊艇

船上生活

berth 名 [bɝθ]（船、火車等的） 床位	cabin 名 [ˋkæbɪn]（船的）客艙	cater to 片 為…服務；迎合
deck 名 [dɛk] 甲板	gangway 名 [ˋgæŋ͵we] 舷梯（供乘客 上下船）	lifeboat 名 [ˋlaɪf͵bot] 救生艇
porthole 名 [ˋport͵hol]（船上的） 圓形窗戶	stateroom 名 [ˋstet͵rum]（輪船、火車 等的）房間	tender 名 [ˋtɛndɚ] 接駁船

063

🔊 **What time's the next boat to Okinawa?**
下一班到沖繩的船是幾點的呢？

🔊 **Would you like a top or bottom berth?**
您想要上舖還是下舖？

🔊 **I'd like a two-berth cabin.**
我想要一間兩床位的艙房。

🔊 **We're two adults and a child, and we'd like a cabin of our own.**
我們有兩位大人和一個小孩，我們想要一間自己的艙房。

🔊 **I prefer a big cabin with an ocean view.**
我比較喜歡有海景的大房間。

🔊 **We don't need a cabin.**
我們不需要艙房。

🔊 **How long does the crossing take?**
航行時間是多久呢？

🔊 **What time does the ferry arrive in Stockholm?**
渡輪什麼時候會抵達斯德哥爾摩？

🔊 **How soon before the departure time do we have to board the boat?**
我們最晚要在出發時間之前多久登船？

🔊 **The ship is fully accessible for disabled travelers.**

這艘船有很多無障礙的設計。

Where's the information desk?
服務台在哪裡呢？

Where's cabin number 258?
二五八號艙房在哪裡呢？

Which deck is the bureau de change on?
外幣兌換處在哪一層呢？

There are three restaurants on board this ship.
這班郵輪上面有三間餐廳。

The next port of call will be Miami.
邁阿密將是我們下一個停靠點。

All car passengers, please make your way down to the car decks for disembarkation.
有帶車的乘客請先去領車，以準備下船。

We will be arriving in port in approximately 30 minutes' time. Please vacate your cabins.
大約三十分鐘後，我們即將抵達港口，請離開您的艙房準備下船。

Sea sickness is a common problem for many first-time travelers on a cruise ship.
很多初次搭遊輪的旅客都會暈船。

The sea's very rough. I feel seasick.
風浪很大，我已經暈船了。

The sea is quite calm today.
今天的風浪很平靜。

Part 3

玩瘋充實行程

Enjoying Your Trip

Start exploring your destination!

都到國外了，當然要體驗一下當地風情！

名 名詞　　動 動詞　　形 形容詞

副 副詞　　介 介係詞　　片 片語　　縮 縮寫

Unit 01 At The Information Center

詢問當地觀光資訊

一定用得到～
3句話搞定旅遊大小事

索取景點手冊

Can I have a brochure?
我可以拿一份景點手冊嗎？

 也能這樣說：

Do you have a pamphlet on sightseeing?
你們有景點手冊嗎？

> **Of course. These brochures are free.**
> 當然，而且這些景點手冊是免費的喔。

詢問推薦景點

What tourist attractions do you recommend?
你會推薦哪些觀光景點呢？

 也能這樣說：

What would you suggest that I visit first?
你建議我先去逛什麼地方呢？

> **Let me see. What type of place are you looking for?**
> 讓我想想，你想去什麼樣的地方呢？

Can I book tickets here?
我可以在這裡預定票券嗎？

也能這樣說：

Can you book the tickets for me?
可以請你幫我預定票券嗎？

Sure. What kind of ticket do you want to book?
可以的，您想要訂哪些票呢？

旅途中也要會的單字　065

 遊客中心

brochure 名 [bro`ʃʊr] 小冊子	**city map** 片 市區地圖	**guidebook** 名 [`gaɪd͵bʊk] 旅行指南
pamphlet 名 [`pæmflɪt] 小冊子	**sightseeing** 名 [`saɪt͵siɪŋ] 觀光	**spot** 名 [spɑt] 旅遊勝地
tourist attraction 片 旅遊勝地	**tourist information/ visitor center** 片 遊客服務中心	**tourist information officer** 片 遊客中心服務員

 景點類型

ancient 形 [`enʃənt] 古代的	**cultural** 形 [`kʌltʃərəl] 文化的	**getaway** 名 [`gɛtə͵we] 出遊
heritage 名 [`hɛrətɪdʒ] 遺產	**historical** 形 [hɪs`tɔrɪkl] 歷史的	**landmark** 名 [`lænd͵mɑrk] 地標
natural 形 [`nætʃərəl] 自然的	**scenic** 形 [`sinɪk] 風景的	**well-traveled** 形 [`wɛl`trævl̩d] 交通繁忙的

Where should we go sightseeing?
我們應該去哪裡觀光呢？

Are there any must-see places in the city?
這個城市有沒有什麼一定要去的地方？

Are you interested in visiting theme parks?
你對主題樂園有沒有興趣？

I don't feel like going to any amusement parks.
我不太想去遊樂園。

I would rather go shopping at outlets.
我寧願到暢貨中心逛街。

What's the best way of getting around the city?
遊覽這個城市最好的方法是什麼？

A **Have you ever visited either Central Park or the Museum of Modern Art?**
你去過中央公園或現代藝術博物館了嗎？

B **No, but I've been meaning to.**
還沒，不過我打算去看看。

A **I'd like to spend one day in Boston.**
我想要在波士頓待一天。

B **Then I suggest you join a day trip.**
那我建議你去參加一日遊。

A visit to Boston must include a walk along the

102

historical Freedom Trail.
到波士頓就一定要去具歷史意義的「自由步道」。

(A) What about the food in Boston?
那波士頓有什麼好吃的東西嗎？

(B) You must try the clam chowder and lobster rolls at Quincy market!
你一定要去吃昆西市場的蛤蠣濃湯和龍蝦堡！

You can't miss New England clam chowder.
你絕對不能錯過新英格蘭風味的蛤蠣濃湯。

We have a list of the top 10 things to do in London. Feel free to take a look!
我們有整理出在倫敦你一定要做的十件事情，看一下這張清單吧！

Here is a guidebook with information about Paris.
這裡有介紹巴黎的旅遊手冊。

There are many places of interest in the city, such as museums and temples.
本市有許多有趣的景點，像是博物館和寺廟。

I highly recommend the night-time tour.
我十分推薦夜間觀光。

The night view of Paris is fantastic!
巴黎的夜景實在是太迷人了！

The Eiffel Tower is lit up at night, and it's amazing.
艾菲爾鐵塔晚上會被照亮，真的很美。

一定用得到～
3句話搞定旅遊大小事

067

詢問特定行程

Is there a tour to Disneyland?
有到迪士尼樂園的團嗎？

也能這樣說：

We are looking for a tour to Disneyland, please.
我們想要找去迪士尼的團。

Absolutely. We also have a tour to Universal Studios.
有的，我們也有到環球影城的團喔。

詢問行程編排

Will we see the Empire State Building?
我們會去帝國大廈嗎？

也能這樣說：

Does this tour cover the Empire State Building?
這個團會參觀帝國大廈嗎？

The tour goes to all the important attractions.
主要的大景點這個團都會去。

詢問其他資訊

Will there be time to to go around by ourselves?
我們有時間可以自己逛逛嗎？

也能這樣說：

Will we have free time when we go to Piazza di Spagna?
我們到西班牙廣場之後會有自由活動時間嗎？

對方可能這樣回應

You will have one hour to go around at each stop.
每一站您都可以自由逛一個小時。

旅途中也要會的單字　068

選擇行程

day trip 片 一日遊	**escorted tour** 片（有領隊的）團體旅遊	**excursion** 名 [ɪk`skɜʒən] 短途旅行
half-day tour 片 半日遊	**incentive trip** 片 員工旅遊	**self-guided tour** 片 自助旅行
tour 名 動 [tʊr] 旅遊	**tour bus** 片 遊覽車	**travel agency/ operator** 片 旅行社

旅遊術語

add on 片 附加服務／產品	**arrangement** 名 [ə`rendʒmənt] 安排	**blackout date** 片 不開團的日期
guide 名 [gaɪd] 導遊	**inclusive** 形 [ɪn`klusɪv] 包含一切費用的	**itinerary** 名 [aɪ`tɪnə,rɛrɪ] 行程；路線
package tour 片 套裝旅遊	**promotion** 名 [prə`moʃən] 促銷	**travel agent** 片 旅行社員工

I was wondering if you could help me book a few tours.
可以請你幫我預訂旅遊團嗎？

How long are you going to stay?
你要在這裡待多久呢？

We have half-day and full-day tours.
我們有半日遊和一日遊的團。

I'd like to join a half-day tour.
我想要參加半日遊。

Do you have a brochure in Chinese?
你們有中文的簡介嗎？

A **What kind of tour do you feel like joining?**
您比較想參加哪一種旅遊團呢？

B **I'm not sure. Which tour would you recommend?**
我還沒決定。你們推薦哪一個團呢？

I can only make it in the morning.
我只能參加早上的團。

A **What historical sites does the tour go to?**
這個團會參觀什麼古蹟嗎？

B **You will be able to visit the ruins of a castle and several ancient monuments.**
會帶您參觀一座城堡遺跡和幾個古代遺址。

Is this a guided tour?
這個團會有導遊嗎？

A What's the difference between tour A and tour B?
行程 A 和行程 B 有什麼不同嗎？

B Tour A is a sightseeing tour while tour B is a shopping tour.
行程 A 以觀光為主，行程 B 則是以購物為主。

Do you have any tours at a discount?
你們有特價中的旅遊團嗎？

Are these temples and shrines worth seeing?
這些寺廟跟神社很值得看嗎？

A This tour package sounds great! How much is it?
這個套裝行程看起來很不錯，費用多少呢？

B It's $120 for one person, and $200 for two.
一個人是一百二十元，兩個人則是兩百元。

A Does your one-day tour include lunch?
一日遊有提供午餐嗎？

B Yes, the fee includes a lunch and a beverage coupon.
有的，團費已包含午餐，還有一張飲料抵用券。

How many people are there in the tour?
一團有多少人呢？

How long does the tour spend at each spot?
每一個景點會停留多久呢？

107

一定用得到～
3句話搞定旅遊大小事

070

問集合時間

When should we get back to the bus?
我們幾點要回巴士那邊集合？

 也能這樣說：

Do you know the time we should meet up on the bus?
你知道幾點要到巴士那邊集合嗎？

> **I think we should all gather up at 4:30.**
> 我記得集合時間是四點半。

對方可能這樣回應

問結束時間

When does the tour finish?
行程幾點結束呢？

 也能這樣說：

What time will the tour finish?
這個行程幾點會結束？

> **We will get back to your hotel before 6 p.m.**
> 我們下午六點前會回到您的飯店。

對方可能這樣回應

請別人拍照

Could you take a picture of us, please?
可以請你幫我們拍個照嗎？

也能這樣說：

Could you take a picture of us with the waterfalls?
可以幫我們連後面的瀑布一起照張相嗎？

對方可能這樣回應

That's no problem.
當然可以。

旅途中也要會的單字 071

 拍照設備

digital camera	flash 名	lens 名
片 數位相機	[flæʃ] 閃光燈	[lɛnz] 相機鏡頭
photo 名	**photograph** 動	**photographer** 名
[`foto] 照片	[`fotə͵græf] 拍照	[fə`tɑgrəfɚ] 攝影師
selfie 名	**selfie stick**	**shoot** 動
[`sɛlfi] 自拍照	片 自拍棒	[ʃut] 拍攝

 一日旅遊

assemble 動	charter 名	day-tripper 名
[ə`sɛmbḷ] 集合；召集	[`tʃɑrtɚ] 包車	[`de͵trɪpɚ] 當天往返的旅客
free time	**gather** 動	**meet up**
片 自由時間	[`gæðɚ] 收集	片 碰面
stop 名	**tour guide**	**tourist trap**
[stɑp] 逗留；停車	片 導遊	片 敲遊客竹槓的地方

還有這些說法～
應急旅遊句會聽也會說

A I'd like to join a Chinese-speaking tour.
我想要參加用中文導覽的團。

B We do have one, but it is fully booked.
我們的確有一團，不過已經額滿了。

A What time does the tour depart?
這個團幾點鐘出發呢？

B Our tour departs at eight in the morning.
早上八點鐘出團。

Will we take a tour bus?
我們會搭遊覽車嗎？

Where should I wait for the tour bus?
我應該要到哪裡等遊覽車？

We will send someone to pick you up at your hotel.
我們會派人到您的飯店接您。

Let's meet at 7:30 a.m. at the lobby of your hotel.
我們約早上七點半，在您的飯店大廳碰面吧。

Hurry up! The tour bus is leaving!
快點！遊覽車要開走了！

Good morning, I am your tour guide. Please call me Henry.
早安！我是你們今天的導遊，叫我亨利就可以了。

A What is Sausalito like?
索薩利托是什麼樣的地方？

B It's a charming small town, just minutes away from the Golden Gate Bridge.
是一個離金門大橋很近的迷人小鎮。

A What's so special about this town?
這個小鎮以什麼著名？

B The town is famous for its breathtaking views.
鎮上美不勝收的風景是最出名的。

Our first stop is downtown Montreal.
我們的第一站是蒙特婁市中心。

Let's enjoy the beautiful view from the top of Montreal Tower!
我們來欣賞從蒙特婁塔頂樓看出去的美景吧！

Is your camera waterproof?
你的相機有防水嗎？

I got ripped-off at that tourist trap.
我被那家黑店敲竹槓了。

I think I'm exhausted. Can we go back to the hotel?
我覺得我已經筋疲力竭了，我們可以回飯店了嗎？

A Should I tip the tour guides?
需要付導遊小費嗎？

B We usually tip the tour guides 10% of the tour price.
我們通常會付團費的百分之十當作小費。

一定用得到～
3句話搞定旅遊大小事

073

問營業時間
What are your hours?
你們的營業時間是從幾點到幾點？

也能這樣說：

What are your hours of operation?
你們的營業時間是從幾點到幾點呢？

It opens from 9 a.m. to 8 p.m. every day.
每天早上九點開門，晚上八點關門。

問活動時間
When does the parade begin?
遊行什麼時候開始？

也能這樣說：

Do you know when the parade will start?
你知道遊行什麼時候開始嗎？

The parade will start at 6 p.m., followed by a fireworks show.
遊行將於晚上六點開始，接下來還有煙火秀。

排隊
排哪裡

Are you lining up for the drop tower?
你們在排隊搭自由落體嗎？

也能這樣說：

Is this the line for the drop tower ride?
請問這是排自由落體的隊伍嗎？

對方可能這樣回應

No. You should line up over there.
不是，你應該排到那邊的隊伍。

旅途中也要會的單字 **074**

 遊樂器材

amusement park 片 遊樂園	**bumper car** 片 碰碰車	**drop tower** 片 自由落體
Ferris wheel 片 摩天輪	**free fall** 片【物】自由落體	**merry-go-round** 名 [`mɛrɪgoˌraund] 旋轉木馬
pirate ship 片 海盜船	**roller coaster** 片 雲霄飛車	**theme park** 片 主題樂園

 各種活動

arcade 名 [ɑr`ked] 長廊商場	**gift shop** 片 紀念品店	**haunted house** 片 鬼屋
parade 名 [pə`red] 遊行	**ride** 名 [raɪd] 遊樂設施	**show** 名 [ʃo] 表演
theme 名 [θim] 主題	**thrill ride** 片 高空遊樂設施總稱	**waterpark** 名 [`watɜˌpark] 水上樂園

113

還有這些說法～
應急旅遊句會聽也會說

📢 I'd like an all-day pass, please.
我要買一日票。

📢 I have a student ID. Let's get student tickets at the ticket booth.
我有學生證，我們去售票亭買學生票吧。

📢 I'd like two adult and two student tickets, please.
我想買兩張全票和兩張學生票。

📢 Here are your passes. Have fun.
這是您的門票，祝您玩得愉快。

📢 Does the pass include everything?
可以用這張票玩所有設施嗎？

📢 I want to go on all the rides.
全部的設施我都想玩。

Ⓐ Look! A roller coaster! Let's take a ride!
你看！有雲霄飛車！我們去玩吧！

Ⓑ I'll pass. The roller coaster ride is too much for me.
我就不坐了，雲霄飛車對我來說太可怕了。

Ⓐ What ride is this amusement park famous for?
這個遊樂園最有名的遊樂設施是哪個？

Ⓑ The roller coaster is the most popular amusement ride here.
雲霄飛車是這裡最熱門的。

Do you want to go on a drop tower?
你要玩自由落體嗎？

A I'd just like to go on something mild, like the merry-go-round.
我只敢玩一些比較不恐怖的，像是旋轉木馬。

B The merry-go-round? Come on! That's for little kids.
旋轉木馬？拜託，那是給小孩子玩的吧！

How about the bumper cars?
要玩碰碰車嗎？

The lines for the Ferris wheel are so long.
摩天輪的隊伍排好長。

All the lines are so long. Where do you want to start?
所有的隊伍都排好長，你想要先玩哪一個？

We should have come earlier to beat the rush.
我們應該早點來，就能避開人潮了。

A How can we get to the pirate ship?
請問海盜船要往哪個方向走？

B It's in section C. You can take a trolley.
它在 C 區，你們可以搭小火車過去。

What is your favorite ride or activity?
你最喜歡的遊樂設施或活動是什麼？

Hey! There's Mickey Mouse! I'm going to take a photo with him.
米老鼠在那裡！我要去跟他合照。

115

Unit 05

Museums, Galleries & Theaters

沾染文藝氣息

一定用得到～
3句話搞定旅遊大小事

詢問入場費

How much is it to get in?
入場費多少錢？

 也能這樣說：

Is there an admission charge?
進場要收費嗎？

> **You only need to pay for the special exhibitions.**
> 只有看特展才需要付費。

對方可能這樣回應

音樂會票券

I'd like four tickets, please.
請給我四張票。

 也能這樣說：

I'd like four tickets to see Les Misérables.
我想買四張《悲慘世界》的票。

> **I'm sorry, it's fully booked.**
> 很抱歉，已經沒有位子了。

對方可能這樣回應

Can I take photographs?
可以照相嗎？

🔊 也能這樣說：

Am I allowed to take photos in here?
館內可以照相嗎？

Yes, but you need to turn off the flash.
可以，但請勿使用閃光燈。

對方可能這樣回應

✈ 旅途中也要會的單字 `077`

 館內設備

admission 名 [əd`mɪʃən] 入場	**box office** 片 票房收入	**cloakroom** 名 [`klok͵rum] 衣帽間
concert hall 片 演藝廳	**gallery** 名 [`gælərɪ] 畫廊；美術館	**no photography** 片 禁止照相
opera house 片 歌劇院	**ticket office** 片 售票處	**theater** 名 [`θiətɚ] 劇院

 藝術欣賞

abstract 形 [`æbstrækt] 抽象的	**art craft** 片 手工藝	**genre** 名 [`ʒɑnrə] 作品類型；流派
modern art 片 現代藝術	**oil painting** 片 油畫	**portrait** 名 [`portret] 肖像；描繪
pottery 名 [`patərɪ] 陶器	**sculpture** 名 [`skʌlptʃɚ] 雕塑品	**watercolor** 名 [`watɚ͵kʌlɚ] 水彩

I'd like two tickets for tomorrow night.
我要買明天晚上的票，請給我兩張。

Ⓐ **What tickets do you have available?**
有哪些票還有賣？

Ⓑ **Sorry, we've got nothing left**
抱歉，所有的票都已經賣完了。

Is there a discount for senior citizens/children?
有老人優待票 / 兒童票嗎？

Ⓐ **Where would you like to sit?**
您想要坐哪裡？

Ⓑ **Near the front/the back./Somewhere in the middle.**
我想要靠前面 / 後面的位子。 / 我想要中間的位子。

Would you like an audio guide?
您想要租語音導覽嗎？

Are there any guided tours today?
今天有導覽嗎？

What time does the next guided tour start?
下一場導覽什麼時候開始？

What time do you close?
你們什麼時候關門呢？

The museum is closed on Mondays.
每週一是博物館的公休日。

118

Where's the cloakroom?
請問衣帽間在哪裡？

Ma'am, you have to leave your bags in the cloakroom.
女士，您必須把背包放到衣帽間裡。

Do you have a plan of the museum?
你們有博物館的樓層簡介嗎？

Who's this painting by?
這幅畫是誰的作品？

Are there any exhibitions on at the moment?
現在有什麼展覽可以看嗎？

Could you tell us what's on at the theater?
請問現在戲院上映的節目是什麼？

Is there anything on at the theater tonight?
請問一下，戲院今晚有什麼節目可觀賞嗎？

When's the play on until?
這齣劇什麼時候結束上映？

A What type of production is it?
這是屬於哪一種類型的戲劇？

B It's a comedy/tragedy.
它是一齣喜劇 / 悲劇。

What time does the performance start/finish?
表演什麼時候開始 / 結束？

Unit 06
Dancing The Night Away

舞動一整夜

一定用得到～
3句話搞定旅遊大小事

079

教人舞步時
Let me show you some simple steps.
我秀一些簡單的舞步給你看。

🔊 也能這樣說：

Let me show you how to dance the waltz.
我來教你怎麼跳華爾滋吧。

Can you move more slowly? I am new to dancing.
你可以慢一點嗎？我是舞蹈初學者。

對方可能這樣回應

負責領舞時
Follow my lead.
跟著我的腳步。

🔊 也能這樣說：

I'll lead you.
我來帶著你跳。

OK. I'll just follow your lead.
好啊，那我就跟著你跳。

對方可能這樣回應

享受
跳舞吧

I like Salsa the most.
我最喜歡騷莎舞了。

也能這樣說：

Salsa is my favorite dance!
我最喜歡騷莎舞了！

Me, too. We have a lot in common!
我也是，我們還真是興趣相投！

對方可能這樣回應

旅途中也要會的單字 080

不同舞風

ballet 名 [`bæle] 芭蕾舞	**belly dance** 片 肚皮舞	**contemporary dance** 片 現代舞
flamenco 名 [flə`mɛnko] 佛朗明哥舞	**salsa** 名 [`salsə] 騷莎舞	**samba** 名 [`sæmbə] 森巴舞
tango 名 [`tæŋgo] 探戈舞	**tap dance** 片 踢踏舞	**waltz** 名 [wɔlts] 華爾滋

享受跳舞

ballroom 名 [`bɔl.rum] 舞廳	**choreograph** 動 [`kɔrɪə.græf] 編舞	**club** 名 [klʌb] 夜店；俱樂部
dance floor 片 舞池	**disco** 名 [`dɪsko] 迪斯可舞廳	**remix** 名 [ri`mɪks] 混音音樂
rhythm 名 [`rɪðəm] 節奏	**step** 名 [stɛp] 踏步	**twist** 名 [twɪst] 扭動

081

🔊 **Come on! Come dancing with us.**
來吧！跟我們一起跳舞吧！

🔊 **The hand movements and steps seem complicated.**
手的動作跟舞步看起來很複雜。

🔊 **Belly dancing is one of the traditional Middle Eastern dances.**
肚皮舞是中東舞蹈的一種。

Ⓐ **I heard that belly dancing can keep you in shape.**
我聽說跳肚皮舞可以保持身材苗條。

Ⓑ **I agree. Belly dancing is a great exercise.**
我同意，肚皮舞是很好的運動。

🔊 **I enjoy twisting and shaking to ancient Middle Eastern rhythms.**
我喜歡隨著古老的中東音樂擺動身體。

🔊 **Dancing the waltz is easy.**
跳華爾滋很簡單。

🔊 **My feet get tangled up all the time when dancing.**
一跳起舞來，我的雙腳就會纏在一起、不聽使喚。

🔊 **Are you ready to dance?**
你準備好要一起跳舞了嗎？

🔊 **May I have the pleasure of dancing with you?**
我有榮幸能和你跳支舞嗎？

122

🔊 **Can I have a dance with you?**
我可以跟你跳支舞嗎？

🔊 **I bet the guy standing there wants to dance with you.**
我很確定站在那邊的男生很想與你共舞。

🔊 **Could we have another dance?**
我們可以再跳一支舞嗎？

🔊 **I feel nervous when going on the dance floor.**
我一踏進舞池裡就很緊張。

Ⓐ **How do you ease your nerves on the dance floor?**
你在舞池都怎麼緩解緊張感呢？

Ⓑ **You can ask your partner to lead.**
你可以請你的舞伴領舞。

🔊 **I enjoy dancing to the beat of the music.**
我喜歡隨著音樂節奏起舞。

🔊 **The D.J. is playing fast songs with strong beats.**
DJ 正在撥放節奏強烈的快歌。

🔊 **I am good at many kinds of dances.**
我對很多舞蹈都很在行。

Ⓐ **Salsa is the best dance in the world, isn't it?**
騷莎是全世界最棒的舞蹈了，不是嗎？

Ⓑ **Right! It's all about having a good time.**
是啊！跳騷莎就是會讓人開心起來。

Unit 07
Social Drinking At The Bar
喝喝小酒互相交流

一定用得到～
3句話搞定旅遊大小事

082

推薦什麼酒

What brand would you recommend?
你推薦哪個牌子呢？

 也能這樣說：

I'd like to try a local beer. What would you suggest?
我想試試本地啤酒，你有什麼推薦的嗎？

> **How about Taiwan Beer? It's very popular here.**
> 台灣啤酒怎麼樣？在這裡很受歡迎喔。

對方可能這樣回應

再來一杯吧

Same again, please.
請再給我一杯同樣的。

 也能這樣說：

Another two beers, please.
麻煩再來兩罐啤酒。

> **Coming up right away.**
> 馬上來。

對方可能這樣回應

點些
食物吃

Do you serve food?
你們有供應食物嗎？

也能這樣說：

Do you have any snacks?
你們有供應點心嗎？

對方可能這樣回應

Yes. We have French fries and fried chicken.
有，我們有薯條和炸雞。

旅途中也要會的單字 `083`

 酒類飲品

ale 名	**beer** 名	**brandy** 名
[el] 麥芽啤酒	[bɪr] 啤酒	[`brændɪ] 白蘭地
cider 名	**gin** 名	**liqueur** 名
[`saɪdɚ] 蘋果酒	[dʒɪn] 琴酒	[lɪ`kɜ] 利口酒
vodka 名	**whisky/whiskey** 名	**wine** 名
[`vɑdkə] 伏特加	[`hwɪskɪ] 威士忌	[waɪn] 葡萄酒

酒吧文化

alcohol 名	**bartender** 名	**cocktail** 名
[`ælkə,hɔl] 酒精	[`bɑr,tɛndɚ] 調酒師	[`kɑk,tel] 雞尾酒
drunk 名	**hangover** 名	**stagger** 動
[drʌŋk] 酒醉的	[`hæŋ,ovɚ] 宿醉	[`stægɚ] 搖搖晃晃
sober 名	**tipsy** 名	**wine glass**
[`sobɚ] 清醒的	[`tɪpsɪ] 微醺的	片 玻璃酒杯

125

084

🔊 **May I see your ID, please?**
我可以看一下您的身分證件嗎？

🔊 **The minimum charge per person is NT$350.**
最低消費是一人三百五十元（新台幣）。

Ⓐ **What would you like to drink, sir? / What can I get you, sir?**
先生，請問您要喝什麼？

Ⓑ **I'll start with some beer. Do you have Porter here?**
我先喝點啤酒，你們有波特啤酒嗎？

🔊 **What kind of beer would you like? We have stout, ale, dry, draft, bitter, and light beers.**
你要什麼種類的啤酒？我們有黑麥啤酒、麥芽啤酒、生啤酒和淡啤酒。（dry/draft beer：酒吧內用大木桶裝的生啤酒）

🔊 **Do you want draft or a bottle?**
您要桶裝生啤酒還是瓶裝啤酒？

🔊 **Bartender! I'll have a martini, please.**
調酒師！來一杯馬丁尼。

🔊 **The cocktail tastes pretty smooth. I like it!**
這杯雞尾酒喝起來很順口，我很喜歡！

🔊 **It's too strong./It's too much for me.**
喝起來太烈了。

🔊 **Whisky on the rocks for me.**

我要威士忌加冰塊。

A What brand of whisky do you want?
您要什麼牌子的威士忌？

B Scotch, straight up.
我要純的蘇格蘭威士忌。

Make mine a double, please.
我要烈一點。

I'll have a glass of V.S.O.P.
我要一杯干邑白蘭地。（V.S.O.P. = Very Superior Old Pale，指酒齡在四年半至六年半間的白蘭地）

What time does the kitchen close?
廚房什麼時候關門？

Are you still serving food?
現在還可以點食物嗎？

Excuse me. What time is your last call?
請問你們的點餐時間最晚到什麼時候？

Do you want some snacks or dessert?
您要一些點心或甜點嗎？

A Do you have any promotions?
你們有什麼優惠活動嗎？

B Our Happy Hour is from 5 p.m. to 6 p.m.
我們的歡樂時光促銷是從晚上五點到六點。

Ladies can get a refill for half-price tonight.
今晚入場的女性若想續杯飲料，全數半價優惠。

Unit
08 Watching Live Sports

現場觀看運動比賽

一定用得到～
3句話搞定旅遊大小事

085

支持哪一隊

Which soccer team do you support?
你支持哪一支足球隊？

🔊 也能這樣說：

Are you a fan of any soccer team?
你有支持哪一支足球隊嗎？

對方可能這樣回應

I'm a huge fan of Real Madrid.
我是皇家馬德里的粉絲。

邀約看比賽

Do you want to go to a baseball game with me?
要不要跟我去看棒球比賽？

🔊 也能這樣說：

Do you want to join me to watch a live baseball game?
你想要跟我去球場看場球賽嗎？

對方可能這樣回應

Only if the Dodgers are playing.
如果是道奇隊的比賽我才去。

128

Which teams are playing?
現在是哪兩隊在比賽呢？

也能這樣說：

Which teams are competing tonight?
今晚的比賽是誰對誰呢？

對方可能這樣回應

It's Italy versus New Zealand.
這場比賽是義大利對紐西蘭。

旅途中也要會的單字   086

欣賞運動

applause 名 [ə`plɔz] 掌聲	**arena** 名 [ə`rinə] 比賽場地	**athlete** 名 [`æθlit] 運動員
field 名 [fild] 運動場	**league** 名 [lig] 聯盟	**movement** 名 [`muvmənt] 動作
sportsmanship 名 [`sportsmən.ʃɪp] 運動家精神	**stadium** 名 [`stedɪəm] 體育場；球場	**tournament** 名 [`tɜnəmənt] 比賽

激烈比賽

champion 名 [`tʃæmpɪən] 冠軍	**coach** 名 [kotʃ] 教練	**competition** 名 [ˌkɑmpə`tɪʃən] 比賽
defense 名 [dɪ`fɛns] 防守	**foul** 名 [faul] （比賽）犯規	**half-time** 名 [`hæf.taɪm]（比賽） 中場休息
offense 名 [ə`fɛns] 進攻	**referee** 名 [ˌrɛfə`ri] 裁判	**score** 動 [skor] 得分

129

Basketball season is right around the corner.
籃球賽季快開始了。

This game is a tug of war between the players.
這兩隊間的比賽激烈，形成拉鋸戰。

It was a close game.
雙方的實力不相上下。

The outcome of the game can still be changed in the last second.
就算只剩一秒鐘，也仍有逆轉比賽結果的可能。

For me, it is very nerve-racking in the final minutes.
球賽最後幾分鐘，我超緊張的。

Let's meet at the front gate of the baseball stadium at 5:30 p.m.
我們五點半約在棒球場的大門碰面吧。

Watching a game at a stadium is a lot of fun.
到球場觀賽非常有趣。

I prefer seats close to center field so that I can see the whole diamond.
我比較喜歡靠近中間走道的座位，因為這樣可以看到整個棒球場。

Do you have any outfield unreserved tickets near left field?
你們有左外野的不劃位票嗎？

🔊 **Did you see the starter on that team?**
你看到那隊的先發投手了嗎？

🔊 **It's a wild pitch, and the ball hit the backstop.**
那是個暴投，球打到了本壘後方的擋球網。

🔊 **It's a grand slam!**
是個滿貫全壘打！

🔊 **Strike out!**
三振出局！

🔊 **The crowd is booing./They are giving a Bronx cheer.**
觀眾噓聲四起。

🔊 **Isn't the World Cup coming up soon?**
世界盃足球賽快開打了吧？

🔊 **Do you follow the World Cup?**
你有看世界盃嗎？

🔊 **The next game is England versus Brazil.**
下一場比賽是英國對巴西。

🔊 **I cannot wait to see the championship final!**
我等不及要看冠軍賽了！

🔊 **Argentina won their opening match 1-0 over Nigeria.**
在開幕賽中，阿根廷以一比零擊敗了奈及利亞隊。

🔊 **How many goals has he scored so far?**
目前為止他得幾分了？

Unit 09

Experiencing Water Sports
體驗水上運動

一定用得到～
3句話搞定旅遊大小事

088

活動有哪些

What can we do at the beach?
我們可以在海灘做什麼呢？

也能這樣說：

What other beach activities can we do?
我們在海邊還能做哪些活動呢？

對方可能這樣回應

You can play beach volleyball or go jet skiing.
你可以玩沙灘排球或騎水上摩托車。

相約潛水去

How about going snorkeling?
要不要去浮潛？

也能這樣說：

Why don't we go snorkeling?
我們何不去浮潛呢？

對方可能這樣回應

Well, I just want to put myself in a chair on the beach and do nothing.
我只想窩在海灘椅上，什麼事都不做。

132

租借海灘器材

Are the beach umbrellas for rent?
那些陽傘是可以租借的嗎？

也能這樣說：

Can we rent the beach umbrella for one hour?
我們可以租一個小時的陽傘嗎？

Sure. It's $2 dollars per hour and $14 dollars for a day.
當然，一小時的租借費為兩元，租一整天的話只要十四元。

對方可能這樣回應

 旅途中也要會的單字 089

海灘必備

bathing suit 片 泳衣	**beach umbrella** 片 陽傘	**flip flop** 片 夾腳拖
rash guard 片 潛水防曬衣	**sun bath** 片 日光浴	**sunburn** 名 [`sʌn͵bɜn] 曬傷
sunglasses 名 [`sʌn͵glæsɪz] 太陽眼鏡	**sunscreen** 名 [`sʌn͵skrin] 防曬乳	**tan** 動 [tæn] 曬成小麥色

水上活動

canoe 名 [kə`nu] 獨木舟	**dive** 動 [daɪv] 潛水	**jet ski** 片 水上摩托車
kayak 名 [`kaɪæk] 獨木舟	**paddle** 動 [`pædl̩] 划；划槳行進	**scuba diving** 片 水肺潛水
snorkeling 名 [`snɔrklɪŋ] 浮潛	**stand up paddling** 片 立槳衝浪	**surf** 動 [sɜf] 衝浪

090

We're going to the beach tomorrow!
我們明天要去海邊！

A Should I bring anything?
我需要帶什麼東西嗎？

B Just wear your bathing suit and relax.
只要穿上泳衣，好好放鬆就行了。

A What is your new bathing suit like? A bikini?
你新泳裝的款式是什麼樣的？比基尼嗎？

B Wearing a bikini? I'm not thin enough.
穿比基尼？我不夠瘦啦！

I always wear a one-piece swimming suit.
我都穿連身式的泳裝。

Wearing flip-flops at the beach is very comfortable.
在沙灘穿夾腳拖很舒服。

A Could you help me apply some sunscreen?
你可以幫我擦防曬乳嗎？

B Sure. I'll put more on your back and neck.
好啊，背上和脖子我會幫你多塗一點。

I am a sun lover. I love taking a sunbath on the sand.
我很愛曬太陽，最喜歡在沙灘上做日光浴。

Let's start tanning. A suntan makes you look healthier.
我們來做日光浴吧，曬成古銅色的肌膚看起來更健康。

How can I get the best tan?
要怎樣曬，才能曬出均勻又漂亮的古銅色呢？

They are grilling in the sun.
他們正在大太陽底下曬著。

You may bring some waterproof sunscreen.
你可以帶一些防水的防曬乳。

Why don't we rent a beach umbrella?
我們去租一把遮陽傘吧。

We can enjoy the summertime under the shade of a beach umbrella.
我們可以躲在遮陽傘下享受夏日時光。

Building sandcastles on the beach is free and fun.
在沙灘蓋沙堡既不用錢又好玩。

A **What if I can't swim?**
如果我不會游泳怎麼辦？

B **Don't worry. You'll have to wear a life jacket when snorkeling.**
別擔心，浮潛時，你必須穿救生衣。

We can swim faster with flippers.
穿上蛙鞋的話，我們就可以游快一點了。

Do you have any beach towels?
你有帶海灘毛巾嗎？

Let's go for a walk on the beach.
我們去海灘上散步吧。

一定用得到～
3句話搞定旅遊大小事

091

想要體驗露營

Can we go camping?
我們可以去露營嗎？

🔊 也能這樣說：

How about adding a camping trip into our itinerary?
我們不妨把露營加進行程裡面，怎麼樣？

> **Sure! That's what I was planning.**
> 好啊，我正想要這樣做呢。

對方可能這樣回應

請別人幫忙

Could you help me pitch the tent?
你能幫我搭帳篷嗎？

🔊 也能這樣說：

Would you mind helping me pitch the tent?
你介意來幫我搭個帳篷嗎？

> **I can certainly do that.**
> 好的，沒問題。

對方可能這樣回應

問場地設備

Are there shower facilities at the campsite?
露營地有淋浴設備嗎？

 也能這樣說：

Does the campground offer shower facilities?
營地有提供淋浴設備嗎？

對方可能這樣回應

It does, but the showers lack privacy.
有是有，但隱密性比較不夠。

旅途中也要會的單字　092

探索戶外

adventure 名 動 [əd`vɛntʃə] 冒險活動	**camp** 名 動 [kæmp] 露營	**earth** 名 [ɝθ] 泥土；地球
explore 動 [ɪk`splor] 探索；探險	**forest** 名 [`fɔrɪst] 森林	**lakeside** 名 [`lek͵saɪd] 湖邊
nature 名 [`netʃə] 大自然	**wilderness** 名 [`wɪldənɪs] 荒野	**wood** 名 [wʊd] 森林；木頭

露營裝備

campsite 名 [`kæmp͵saɪt] 露營地	**facility** 名 [fə`sɪlətɪ] 設備	**headlamp** 名 [`hɛd͵læmp] 頭燈
picnic 名 [`pɪknɪk] 野餐	**sleeping bag** 片 睡袋	**sweatshirt** 名 [`swɛt͵ʃɝt] 長袖運動衫
tent 名 [tɛnt] 帳篷	**water bottle** 片 水壺	**waterproof** 形 [`wɔtə͵pruf] 防水的

I found a scenic place. Let's go camping there.
我發現了一個風景幽美的地方，我們去那裡露營吧。

Are there lots of good spots to take pictures?
那裡適合拍照的地方多嗎？

Don't forget to apply insect repellent.
別忘了擦防蚊液。

You might encounter some insects or snakes around your camping area.
營地附近可能會有昆蟲和蛇。

There you go! This hot dog is ready to eat.
好了！熱狗已經可以吃了。

I've brought some beer to go with hot dogs.
我帶了一些啤酒要來配熱狗。

The beer is in the cooler.
啤酒在冰桶裡。

The scenery around the new campground is breathtaking.
這個新露營區的風景真是美呆了。

The campground is always crowded and cramped during weekends.
週末假日的時候，這個營區總是被擠得水洩不通。

📢 **We can unpack and start to set up camp.**
我們可以卸下裝備，開始準備露營了。

Ⓐ **We are going to build a campfire.**
我們要生營火了。

Ⓑ **Awesome! A campfire has long been a symbol of camping.**
太棒了！營火一直都是露營的象徵。

📢 **Starting a campfire can be a bit challenging.**
生營火頗具挑戰性。

📢 **We can use the campfire to cook when camping.**
我們露營時可以用營火來煮東西。

📢 **Cooking food is one of the most enjoyable camping traditions.**
在露營必備的慣例活動中，烹煮食物是最有趣的了。

📢 **A good Swiss Army Knife is a must-bring when going camping.**
去露營時，一定要帶把好用的瑞士刀。

Ⓐ **What camp food do we have?**
我們有哪些露營食物？

Ⓑ **We have some ready-to-eat camp food, such as cheese and crackers.**
我們有一些不用煮的露營食物，像是起司和餅乾。

📢 **The fire needs tending.**
誰去顧一下營火吧。

📢 **How was it? Was it fun?**
怎麼樣？好玩嗎？

一定用得到～
3句話搞定旅遊大小事

問可否換匯

Do you exchange foreign currency?
你們有提供換匯嗎？

 也能這樣說：

Can I exchange foreign currency at this post office?
我可以在這間郵局兌換外幣嗎？

> **Yes, you can exchange your money here.**
> 可以，我們這邊可以換匯。

對方可能這樣回應

詢問匯率時

What is your exchange rate for the Euro?
歐元現在的匯率是多少？

 也能這樣說：

What's the exchange rate for the New Taiwan dollar to the Euro?
請問一下台幣對歐元的匯率是多少？

> **The exchange rate for the Euro is NT$35 for every Euro.**
> 目前每三十五元新台幣可以換一歐元。

對方可能這樣回應

140

麻煩
換外幣

I'd like to change some money.
我想要換匯。

也能這樣說：

I'd like to change some Euro into U.S. dollars.
我想要把歐元換成美金。

對方可能這樣回應

Sure. How much would you like to change?
沒問題。你想要換多少錢呢？

旅途中也要會的單字 **095**

 換匯相關

bill 名	**check/cheque** 名	**currency** 名
[bɪl]（美）紙鈔	[tʃɛk]（美／英）支票	[`kɝənsɪ] 貨幣
currency market 片 外匯交易市場	**denomination** 名 [dɪˌnɑməˋneʃən]（貨幣等的）面額	**exchange rate** 片 匯率
foreign exchange 片 外匯	**note** 名 [not]（英）紙鈔	**traveler's check** 片 旅行支票

 常見外幣

Euro 名	**Japanese Yen**	**Korean Won**
[`juro] 歐元	片 日幣	片 韓元
New Taiwan dollar 片 新台幣	**pound** 名 [paund] 英鎊	**Renminbi (RMB)** 名 [`rɛn`mɪn`bi] 人民幣
Swiss Franc 片 瑞士法郎	**Thai Baht** 片 泰銖	**U.S. dollar** 片 美元

096

📢 Different bureau de change will offer different exchange rates.
每一間換匯所的匯率都不一樣。

📢 I suggest that you don't exchange currencies at the airport.
我建議你不要在機場換匯。

📢 What is the minimum amount of money I should change?
我最少要換多少錢？

Ⓐ I'd like to order some foreign currency.
我想要換一些外幣。
Ⓑ What currency do you want?
您要換什麼貨幣呢？

📢 I'd like some U.S. dollars.
我想換一些美元。

📢 What's the exchange rate for the Japanese Yen?
台幣對日元的匯率是多少呢？

Ⓐ What's the selling rate for the Euro?
歐元的賣價是少？
Ⓑ 1.19 U.S. dollars to the Euro.
一點一九美元可兌換一歐元。

📢 How much is NT$1,000 currently worth in U.S. dollars?

新台幣一千元可以兌換多少美金呢？

A How would you like the money?
您要兌換多少元的面額呢？

B In tens, please.
請給我十元的鈔票。

A Would you like it in any specific denomination?
您有特別想要換什麼面額的鈔票嗎？

B A hundred dollars in twenties and the rest in hundred dollar bills, please.
其中一百元換二十元的面額，剩下的都換百元鈔。

Could you give me some smaller notes?
可以給我面額小一點的鈔票嗎？

What denominations of foreign currency can I order?
我能兌換的面額有哪些呢？

A Have you got any identification?
您有帶身分證件嗎？

B I've got my passport.
我有帶護照。

Are there any foreign exchange ATMs?
這裡有外幣提款機嗎？

Where's the nearest cash machine?
離這邊最近的提款機在哪裡呢？

Can I have a receipt?
可以給我收據嗎？

一定用得到～
3句話搞定旅遊大小事

問郵票 價錢

How much will it cost to send this postcard to Taiwan?
寄明信片到台灣要花多少錢？

也能這樣說：

How much do I have to put on the postcard from the USA to Taiwan?
從美國寄明信片到台灣要花多少錢？

對方可能這樣回應

A postcard sent worldwide by airmail is $1.15.
寄到世界各地的郵票都是一塊錢十五分。

說明寄 信地點

I'd like to send this to Taiwan.
我想要寄到台灣。

也能這樣說：

I'd like to send this postcard to Taiwan.
我想要寄這張明信片到台灣。

對方可能這樣回應

OK. That'll be $1.15.
好的，這樣是一塊錢十五分。

問販售物品

Do you sell postcards?
你們有賣明信片嗎？

也能這樣說：

Can I buy postcards here?
這裡有賣明信片嗎？

Sure. They are placed on a display rack over there.
有，在那邊的展示架上面。

對方可能這樣回應

旅途中也要會的單字
098

郵件相關

airmail 名 [`ɛr, mel] 航空郵件	**mail** 動 [mel] 郵寄	**parcel** 名 [`pɑrs!] 包裹
postage 名 [`postɪdʒ] 郵資	**postbox** 名 [`post, bɑks] 郵筒	**postcard** 名 [`post, kard] 明信片
post office 片 郵局	**stamp** 名 [stæmp] 郵票	**tracking number** 片（郵件）追蹤號碼

寄送服務

domestic express mail 片 國內快捷郵件	**express mail** 片 快捷郵件	**express mail service (EMS)** 片 快捷郵件服務
international express mail 片 國際快捷郵件	**postmark** 名 [`post, mark] 郵戳	**prompt delivery mail** 片 急件
registered mail 片 掛號信	**regular mail** 片 普通郵件	**stamp collecting** 片 集郵

145

Could I have some stamps, please?
請給我幾張郵票。

How many stamps would you like?
您要買幾張郵票呢？

How much is a first-class stamp?
一般郵票多少錢呢？

I'd like an envelope, please.
請給我一個信封。

I want to send the parcel to Taiwan by airmail.
我想用航空郵件寄這件包裹到台灣。

How much does it cost to send this letter to Germany by EMS?
請問這封信用快捷郵件服務寄到德國要多少錢呢？

Can you put it on the scales, please?
麻煩把它放到秤上。

How long does international mail take?
請問寄國際郵件需要多久時間呢？

Where's the postbox?
郵筒在哪裡呢？

What's the last date I can post this to Australia to arrive in time for Christmas?

卡片要在聖誕節之前到澳洲的話，最晚什麼時候要寄出？

A Don't forget to send me a postcard when you visit Canada.
到加拿大玩的時候別忘了寄明信片給我喔。

B Sure. I will. I love to send postcards to friends when I travel.
當然，我會的。我旅行時很愛寄明信片給朋友們。

I usually buy postcards with pictures of tourist attractions on them.
我經常會買印有景點的明信片。

I don't like to send postcards because it's not easy to find a post office during my trips.
我不喜歡寄明信片，因為在旅程中不容易找到郵局。

You can buy stamps at a stamp vending machine.
你可以在郵票販賣機買郵票。

I want to buy some stamps. Which line should I be in?
我想要買郵票，那我應該排哪裡才對呢？

I'd like to buy four NT$5 dollar stamps, please.
我想要買四張新台幣五元的郵票。

I want to send this letter to Spain. How long does it take?
我想要寄這封信去西班牙，請問需要多久時間呢？

Unit 13 Making Phone Calls

撥打國際或國內電話

一定用得到～
3句話搞定旅遊大小事

電話開頭　Hi, this is Thomas. I'd like to speak to Lisa, please.
你好，我是湯姆斯，請幫我接莉莎。

 也能這樣說：

Hi, it's Thomas speaking. May I speak to Lisa?
你好，我是湯姆斯，請問莉莎在嗎？

Hold on, please. I'll put you through.
請稍等，我把電話轉給她。

撥打國際電話　International phone call to Taiwan, please.
請幫我打國際電話到台灣。

 也能這樣說：

I'd like to make an international phone call to Taiwan.
我想打通國際電話到台灣。

Please tell me the person's phone number and name.
請告訴我對方的號碼和姓名。

148

詢問國
際代碼

Country for Taiwan, please?
請問台灣的國際代碼是幾號？

 也能這樣說：

What's the country code for Taiwan?
台灣的國際代碼是幾號呢？

對方可能這樣回應

The country code is 886.
國碼是 886。

 旅途中也要會的單字 〔101〕

🗺 電話禮儀

answer 名 動	**dial** 動	**hang up**
[`ænsə] 回答	[`daɪəl] 撥號；打電話	片 掛斷電話
hold 動	**leave a message**	**long-distance** 形
[hold] 不掛電話	片 留言	[`lɔŋ`dɪstəns] 長途的
make a (phone) call	**put sb. through**	**ring** 動
片 打電話	片 為某人接通電話	[rɪŋ] 打電話

🗺 電話設備

area code	**collect call**	**cordless** 形
片 區碼	片 由受話人付費的電話	[`kɔrdlɪs] 不用電線的
country code	**local call**	**payphone** 名
片 國碼	片 本地電話	[`pefon] （投幣式）公共電話
pound key	**star key**	**voice mail**
片 井字鍵	片 米字鍵	片 語音信箱

A Is there a payphone nearby?
這附近有公共電話嗎？

B You can find a payphone in the hotel lobby.
旅館大廳有一台公共電話。

How can I make a phone call with this card?
我要怎麼用這張電話卡打電話呢？

Can you break this $100 bill into smaller bills, please?
我可以用這張百元鈔跟你換零錢嗎？

A Can I use this phone?
我可以用這個電話嗎？

B Sure, go ahead.
當然可以，請用。

Can you tell me how to make a call to Taiwan?
請問要怎麼打電話到台灣呢？

I don't have any money with me. I'd like to make a collect call.
我沒帶錢，想打對方付費的電話。

Do you know how to dial a collect call?
你知道怎麼打對方付費的電話嗎？

Do you mind if I use your cell phone? I just need to make a quick call.
你介意我借你的手機打通電話嗎？很快就會還你。

150

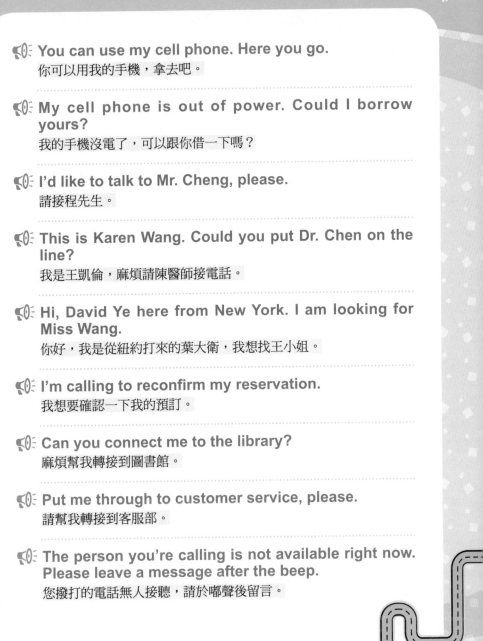

📣 You can use my cell phone. Here you go.
你可以用我的手機，拿去吧。

📣 My cell phone is out of power. Could I borrow yours?
我的手機沒電了，可以跟你借一下嗎？

📣 I'd like to talk to Mr. Cheng, please.
請接程先生。

📣 This is Karen Wang. Could you put Dr. Chen on the line?
我是王凱倫，麻煩請陳醫師接電話。

📣 Hi, David Ye here from New York. I am looking for Miss Wang.
你好，我是從紐約打來的葉大衛，我想找王小姐。

📣 I'm calling to reconfirm my reservation.
我想要確認一下我的預訂。

📣 Can you connect me to the library?
麻煩幫我轉接到圖書館。

📣 Put me through to customer service, please.
請幫我轉接到客服部。

📣 The person you're calling is not available right now. Please leave a message after the beep.
您撥打的電話無人接聽，請於嘟聲後留言。

Part 4

手提大包小包

Time To Go Shopping

Be sure to bring your friends and family some souvenirs!

搜刮紀念品的同時，也要記得買禮物送家人朋友喔！

名 名詞　　動 動詞　　形 形容詞

副 副詞　　介 介係詞　　片 片語　　縮 縮寫

Unit 01

Going Grocery Shopping

採買食品雜貨

一定用得到～
3句話搞定旅遊大小事

尋找物品時

Where can I get the canned tuna?
請問哪裡有鮪魚罐頭？

🔊 也能這樣說：

Excuse me. Which aisle can I find canned tuna in?
請問鮪魚罐頭放在哪條走道呢？

對方可能這樣回應

The canned foods are on the second shelf in aisle nine.
罐頭都放在九號走道的第二個架子上。

問有無特價

What sales on produce do you have today?
你們的農產品今天有什麼在特價嗎？

🔊 也能這樣說：

Do you know what produce is on sale?
你知道有什麼農產品在特價嗎？

對方可能這樣回應

I don't know. The produce person can tell you, though.
我不清楚，但負責農產品區的店員應該知道。

154

Do you have more flour in the back?
請問麵粉還有貨嗎？

也能這樣說：

Do you have this item in stock?
你們倉庫還有這個嗎？

對方可能這樣回應

Wait a second, please. Let me check for you.
請稍等，我替您確認一下。

✈ **旅途中也要會的單字** 104

超商裡面

aisle 名 [aɪl] 走道	**automatic checkout** 片 自助結帳檯	**basket** 名 [`bæskɪt] 籃子
express checkout 片 快速結帳檯	**grocery store** 片 雜貨店	**plastic bag** 片 塑膠袋
reusable bag 片 環保袋	**shopping cart** 片 購物推車	**supermarket** 名 [`supɚˏmɑrkɪt] 超市

食品分類

bakery 名 [`bekərɪ] 烘焙食品	**canned food** 片 罐頭食品	**condiment** 名 [`kɑndəmənt] 調味料
dairy 名 [`dɛrɪ] 乳製品	**deli** 名 [`dɛlɪ] 熱食	**ethnic/imported food** 片 進口食品
frozen food 片 冷凍食品	**household item** 片 家庭用品	**produce** 名 [`prɑdjus] 農產品

105

Do you have your shopping list with you?
你有帶購物清單嗎？

A How much are the tomatoes?
番茄怎麼賣？

B Six for NT$60. They are really fresh.
六個六十元，它們很新鮮喔。

The price shown on the tag is for 100g.
標籤上標的是每一百克的價錢。

Look! Cherries are on sale now.
你看！櫻桃在特價耶。

Bananas are in season now.
香蕉是當季水果。

Why don't we buy a couple slices of ham for breakfast?
我們買幾片火腿當早餐吧。

Let's head to the meat department.
我們到肉品區看看吧。

I want some steak and veal cutlets, please.
麻煩給我一些牛排和牛肉片。

Could you get the shrimps weighed?
可以幫我秤一下這些蝦子嗎？

The butter isn't here. Where can I find it?
奶油不在這裡，放在哪裡呢？

There're some free samples. Let's try some.
那邊有一些試吃品，我們去試吃吧。

Let's move to the cashier's desk.
我們去結帳吧。

Maybe we should go to the self-checkout counter.
或許我們該到自助結帳檯結帳。

May I use the coupons?
我可以使用折價券嗎？

A How much did the bill come to?
總共多少錢呢？

B It comes to NT$2,102 in total.
總共是新台幣兩千一百零二元。

A Do you need a shopping bag?
您需要購物袋嗎？

B No, we've got our own bag.
不用了，我們有自備袋子。

Do you want to pay by cash or credit card?
請問您要付現還是刷卡？

Do you have a membership?
您有本店的會員資格嗎？

Unit 02 Shopping For Cosmetics

化妝品及保養品

一定用得到～
3句話搞定旅遊大小事

106

詢問適合產品

Do you have anything for oily skin?
你們有適合油性肌膚的產品嗎？

 也能這樣說：

Hi, I'm looking for toners suitable for oily skin.
你好，我想要找適合油性肌膚的化妝水。

> We do have the right toner for you. Would you like some samples?
> 我們有適合您的化妝水，您要一些試用品嗎？

問可否試用

Can I sample the lipstick?
我可以試塗口紅嗎？

 也能這樣說：

Do you have any testers for this lipstick color?
你們有這款口紅顏色的試用品嗎？

> Yes, of course. Here is a tester.
> 當然，試用品在這裡。

158

請對方示範

Could you demonstrate how to apply it?
可以示範一下怎麼用嗎？

◀ 也能這樣說：

Could you show me how to apply a concealer for my dark circles?
可以示範一下怎麼用遮瑕膏蓋掉黑眼圈嗎？

對方可能這樣回應

Sure. Do you want me to apply it to your face?
當然可以，需要我直接幫您上妝嗎？

 旅途中也要會的單字 107

 認識臉部

cheek 名 [tʃik] 臉頰	**cheek bone** 片 顴骨	**cosmetic** 名 [kɑz`mɛtɪk] 化妝品（常用複數 cosmetics）
eyebrow 名 [`aɪˌbraʊ] 眉毛	**eyelid** 名 [`aɪˌlɪd] 眼皮	**forehead** 名 [`fɔrˌhɛd] 額頭
lip 名 [lɪp] 嘴脣	**makeup** 名 [`mekˌʌp] 化妝品	**nasal bridge** 片 鼻梁

化妝及保養

eyeliner 名 [`aɪˌlaɪnɚ] 眼線筆	**eye shadow** 片 眼影	**face powder** 片 蜜粉
foundation 名 [faʊn`deʃən] 粉底	**lipstick** 名 [`lɪpˌstɪk] 口紅	**lotion** 名 [`loʃən] 乳液
mascara 名 [mæs`kærə] 睫毛膏	**skin care** 片 護膚	**toner** 名 [`tonɚ] 化妝水

A May I help you with any of the Chanel products?
請問您要找香奈兒的什麼產品呢？

B I want to buy their waterproof mascara.
我想買香奈兒的防水睫毛膏。

A Is it for yourself or for someone else?
您自己要用的還是要送人的？

B It's for myself, please.
我自己要用的，麻煩了。

📢 Would you like to try this hydration active moisture boost?
您要不要試用這款深層保濕精華液呢？

A I am looking for a face cream for my mother.
我想要買面霜給我媽媽。

B Does she use any particular brand?
她有習慣使用的品牌嗎？

📢 What is so special about it?
這個有什麼特別的功效嗎？

📢 Can anti-wrinkle cream really help you get rid of wrinkles?
抗皺霜真的可以消除皺紋嗎？

📢 This concealer covers freckles and pimples. It can even out your skin tone, too.
這款遮瑕膏可以用來遮雀斑和痘痘，還能平衡膚色。

160

The perfect liquid foundation protects you from ultraviolet rays.
這瓶完美的粉底液能抵擋紫外線。

The powder matches your complexion perfectly.
這款蜜粉跟你的膚色很搭。

A Do you use mascara?
您有使用睫毛膏的習慣嗎？

B I don't use mascara much because I don't know how to remove it.
我不常用，因為我不知道怎麼卸掉睫毛膏。

This counter girl can show you how to apply eyeliner.
這位專櫃小姐可以教您怎麼畫眼線。

I would recommend that you wear waterproof mascara if you wear contact lenses.
如果您戴隱形眼鏡，我會推薦您用防水睫毛膏。

A Where can I buy an eyelash curler?
哪裡可以買到睫毛夾呢？

B Eyelash curlers can be found in the beauty and makeup sections of any drug store or grocery store.
在藥妝店或超級市場的美容化妝區，都可以找到睫毛夾。

Where did you buy your eye shadow?
你的眼影是在哪裡買的？

Can I have some samples for this wash off mask?
我可以拿一些水洗式面膜的試用品嗎？

一定用得到～
3句話搞定旅遊大小事

109

詢問尺寸時

Do you have any smaller/larger sizes?
這件有小 / 大一點的尺寸嗎？

也能這樣說：

Do you have this in a smaller/larger size, please?
請問這件有小 / 大一點的尺寸嗎？

Yes, here you are.
有的，在這邊。

業對方可能這樣回應

想找不同顏色

Do you have it in pink?
這件有粉紅色的款示嗎？

也能這樣說：

Does it come in any other colors?
這件有沒有別的顏色？

I am sorry, all the other colors are out of stock.
很抱歉，其他顏色目前都缺貨。

業對方可能這樣回應

162

問在哪裡試穿

Where can I try it on?
哪裡可以試穿呢？

也能這樣說：

Where are the changing rooms, please?
請問更衣室在哪裡？

對方可能這樣回應

Here. Follow me, please.
請往這邊走。

旅途中也要會的單字 110

 熱門顏色

amber 名 [`æmbə] 橙黃色；琥珀色	**army green** 片 軍綠色	**dark** 形 [dɑrk] 深色的
ivory 名 [`aɪvərɪ] 象牙色	**khaki** 名 [`kɑkɪ] 卡其色	**light** 形 [laɪt] 淡色的
mustard 名 [`mʌstəd] 芥末黃	**navy** 名 [`nevɪ] 海軍藍	**scarlet** 名 [`skɑrlɪt] 猩紅色

 挑選衣服

boutique 名 [buˋtik] 時裝店；精品店	**changing/fitting room** 片 試衣間	**fit** 動 [fɪt]（衣服）合身
hanger 名 [`hæŋə] 衣架	**mannequin** 名 [`mænəkɪn] 人體模型	**measurement** 名 [`mɛʒəmənt] 尺寸
shelf 名 [ʃɛlf] 架子	**size** 名 [saɪz] 尺寸	**try on** 片 試穿

Excuse me. Where can I find women's wear?
不好意思，請問女裝部在哪裡？

A Are you looking for anything in particular?
您在找什麼商品嗎？

B No, thanks. I'm just looking.
沒有，我只是隨便看看。

I'm looking for something in season.
我正在找當季商品。

I need a dress for a wedding party.
我在找婚禮可以穿的洋裝。

A Are you looking for a particular color?
您有要找特定的顏色嗎？

B I prefer a suit-dress in white or beige.
我喜歡白色或米色的正式裙裝。

Is this the only color?
只有這個顏色嗎？

I'd like to check out this pencil skirt, too.
我也想看一下這件窄裙。

A Does it come in plaid?
這件有格子圖案的嗎？

B No, just polka dot.
沒有，這件只有圓點圖案的。

Do you have a different pattern or style?
有沒有跟這件不同的圖案或樣式？

I'm not sure what size I am in the British size system. Do you have a size conversion chart?
我不確定換成英式尺寸，我要穿幾號，你們有尺寸的轉換表嗎？

Do you have it in size 10, please?
這件衣服有十號的嗎？

Could you find this in size 4, please?
麻煩幫我找這件的四號。

Would you like me to take your measurements?
需要我幫您量尺寸嗎？

A **What size do you usually wear?**
您通常都穿什麼尺碼的衣服？

B **I usually wear a medium.**
我通常都穿 M 號。

I think this uniform is a little small. What size is this?
我覺得這件制服有點小，這件幾號呢？

Can I have the next size up/down?
可以拿大一號 / 小一號的尺寸嗎？

Is this cardigan machine washable?
這件羊毛衫可以用洗衣機洗嗎？

How should I care for this suit?
我要怎樣保養這套西裝呢？

一定用得到～
3句話搞定旅遊大小事

問當季
鞋款

What is in this autumn?
今年秋天流行哪些款式？

也能這樣說：

Are there any must-buys this season?
有沒有這季必買的款式呢？

對方可能這樣回應

Well, slip-on shoes and combat
boots are all the rage this year.
今年很流行懶人鞋和軍靴喔。

試穿
鞋子

Can I try these shoes on?
我可以試穿這雙鞋嗎？

也能這樣說：

Is it okay if I try these on?
我可以試穿這雙鞋嗎？

對方可能這樣回應

Sure. What size do you usually
wear?
好的，您通常穿幾號鞋？

決定
買這雙

I'll take these.
我要買這雙。

<)) 也能這樣說：

I'll have these, please.
我要買這雙鞋，麻煩了。

OK. How would you like to pay?
好的，您要怎麼結帳呢？

 旅途中也要會的單字 **113**

常見鞋類

boot 名 [but] 靴子	**dress shoe** 片 皮鞋	**high heel** 片 高跟鞋
loafer 名 [`lofə] 平底鞋；樂福鞋	**platform** 名 [`plæt͵fɔrm] 厚底鞋	**sandal** 名 [`sændl] 涼鞋
slip-on shoe 片 懶人鞋	**sneaker** 名 [`snikə] 運動鞋	**wedge** 名 [wɛdʒ] 楔形鞋

風格與組成

heel 名 [hil] 鞋跟	**insole** 名 [`ɪn͵sol] 鞋墊	**leather** 形 [`lɛðə] 皮革製的
oxford 名 [`ɑksfəd] 牛津鞋	**pointed** 形 [`pɔɪntɪd] 尖頭的	**shoelace** 名 [`ʃu͵les] 鞋帶
sole 名 [sol] 鞋底	**vamp** 名 [væmp] 鞋面	**Velcro** 名 [`vɛlkro] 魔鬼氈

114

I am looking for a pair of shoes for a formal dinner party.
我想要找正式晚宴可以穿的鞋子。

I need something to go with my light blue dress.
我需要找雙能搭配我那套淺藍色洋裝的鞋子。

Do you want pumps or sandals?
您要找包鞋還是涼鞋呢？

A **Do you prefer a round toe or a square toe?**
您喜歡圓頭還是方頭的鞋款呢？

B **I want to check out both.**
我兩種都想看一下。

A **I'm afraid that my feet are too wide to wear them.**
我怕我的腳太寬，會穿不下。

B **If you have wide feet, you should get a larger size.**
如果您的腳掌比較寬，可以選大一號的尺寸。

Why don't you try them on and walk around in them.
您不妨試穿，走幾步感受一下。

A **What size of shoes do you wear?**
您都穿幾號的鞋呢？

B **My shoe size is typically 7, but sometimes 6.5.**
我大部分都穿七號，有時候會穿到六號半。

The shoes are a bit loose.
這雙鞋有點鬆。

A Can I try the larger/smaller one, please?
我可以試穿大一號 / 小一號的鞋嗎？

B OK. Let me get a larger/smaller size for you.
好的，我拿大一號 / 小一號的鞋給您。

Do you have anything bigger/smaller?
有大一點 / 小一點的尺寸嗎？

This pair of shoes is just my size.
這雙鞋我穿起來剛剛好。

The pair of boots looks nice. Are they on sale?
這雙靴子很好看，有特價嗎？

A I am looking for a pair of loafers for my husband.
我在幫我先生找一雙平底鞋。

B I recommend this pair. They are the latest.
我會推薦這雙最新款的鞋子。

What style does your husband prefer?
您先生喜歡什麼款式的鞋子呢？

What size does he wear?
他穿幾號鞋呢？

A Where are they made?
這雙鞋是哪裡製造的？

B They were made in Spain.
是西班牙製的。

Is there any other color available?
還有其他顏色嗎？

169

Unit 05 Buying Souvenirs & Gifts

購買當地特產

一定用得到～
3句話搞定旅遊大小事

115

店員推薦購買
Is there anything you can recommend?
請問有什麼推薦的商品嗎？

也能這樣說：

Can you please help me choose a nice souvenir?
可以幫我挑一下合適的紀念品嗎？

> ### Sure. What type of things do you like?
> 好的，您喜歡什麼樣的東西呢？

對方可能這樣回應

特色紀念品
What is the most popular souvenir here in Japan?
在日本，什麼紀念品是最受歡迎的呢？

也能這樣說：

I'm looking for something with a local flavor.
我想買有本地特色的東西。

> ### How about Omamori or matcha?
> 御守或抹茶您覺得如何？

對方可能這樣回應

Do you have a box for the bracelet?
你們有盒子能裝這個手環嗎？

也能這樣說：

Could you put the bracelet into a gift box?
可以幫我用禮物盒包裝這個手環嗎？

No problem. There you go.
沒問題。這是您的手環。

旅途中也要會的單字 116

 送禮選擇

gift-wrap 動 [`gɪft͵ræp] 用包裝紙包裝	**handmade** 形 [`hænd͵med] 手工的	**local** 形 [`lokl] 當地的
relic 名 [`rɛlɪk] 紀念物；遺跡	**remembrance** 名 [rɪ`mɛmbrəns] 紀念品；紀念	**souvenir** 名 [`suvə͵nɪr] 紀念品；伴手禮
token 名 [`tokən] 紀念品；象徵	**unique** 形 [ju`nik] 獨特的	**wrap** 動 [ræp] 包裝

 各種紀念品

badge 名 [bædʒ] 徽章	**cap** 名 [kæp] 帽子	**flag** 名 [flæg] 旗子
key chain/ring 片 鑰匙圈	**magnet** 名 [`mægnɪt] 磁鐵	**mug** 名 [mʌg] 馬克杯
notebook 名 [`not͵bʊk] 筆記本	**ornament** 名 [`ɔrnəmənt] 裝飾品	**snow dome** 片 雪花球

171

Where can I find a gift shop? I didn't see one anywhere.
哪裡有禮品店呢？我在這附近都沒有看到。

I want to get some souvenirs for my friends.
我想要買一些紀念品送朋友。

A Do you sell any souvenirs here?
你們有賣紀念品嗎？

B Yes, we do. Is there anything in particular you're looking for?
有的，您有想找什麼特定的物品嗎？

A Do you have any local souvenirs in mind to recommend?
你推薦我買哪種本地紀念品呢？

B We have a lot of locally-made items. How about the handmade coin purse?
我們有賣很多本地製作的東西，手作零錢包您覺得如何？

A What's your budget for the gifts for your friends?
您送禮的預算大概多少呢？

B I hope the total cost can be below $100.
我希望總價格能壓在一百元美金以下。

A The Mickey dolls are cute. Maybe I can get one for my nephew.
這些米老鼠玩偶好可愛喔，或許可以買來送我姪子。

B Good choice! That's our most popular souvenir.
好選擇！那是我們這裡最受歡迎的紀念品呢。

The souvenirs are so expensive! I didn't expect this.
我沒有想到這裡的紀念品都這麼貴！

I will only get some postcards for my friends.
我只要買些明信片給我朋友就好了。

These magnets look good. I'll get some.
這些磁鐵看起來還不錯，我買幾個好了。

The gift shop is a tourist trap.
這間禮品店根本就是在敲竹槓。

I'd like to buy a teddy bear for my niece.
我想買隻泰迪熊給我姪女。

Can I have it, please?
我要這個，麻煩了。

I'll get it. Could you wrap it in bubble wrap for me?
我買這個好了，可以幫我裝泡泡袋裡面嗎？

I want this pair of ear rings. Can you take off the price tag?
我要買這副耳環，可以幫我把價格標籤拆掉嗎？

Shall I gift-wrap it?
要幫您包裝嗎？

I'd like it to be wrapped as a gift.
請幫我用禮物紙包裝。

Do you want me to put them in a box?
要幫您裝在盒子裡面嗎？

Unit
06 Getting The Best Price & Making Payments

結帳難免討價還價

一定用得到～
3句話搞定旅遊大小事

118

算便宜
一點

Will it be cheaper if I buy two sets?
買兩組的話，可以算便宜一點嗎？

🔊 也能這樣說：

Can you lower the price if I buy two sets?
如果我買兩組，可以算我便宜一點嗎？

If you buy two gift sets, I can give you an extra five percent off.
如果您買兩組禮盒，就可以再幫您打九五折。

對方可能這樣回應

想要
結帳時

Where is the checkout?
請問結帳櫃檯在哪裡？

🔊 也能這樣說：

Where do I pay?
哪裡可以結帳呢？

You can pay in the front.
您可以到前面櫃檯結帳。

對方可能這樣回應

174

選擇結帳方式

Do you accept credit cards?
你們收信用卡嗎？

也能這樣說：

Can I pay with a credit card?
可以用信用卡付錢嗎？

對方可能這樣回應

Yes. We accept all major credit cards.
可以，很多信用卡我們都收。

旅途中也要會的單字

119

準備結帳

cash 名 [kæʃ] 現金；錢	**cashier** 名 [kæˋʃɪr] 收銀員	**checkout** 名 [ˋtʃɛk͵aʊt] 付款處
clearance item 片 清倉商品	**counter** 名 [ˋkaʊntɚ] 櫃檯	**credit card** 片 信用卡
negotiation 名 [nɪ͵goʃɪˋeʃən] 談判；交涉	**pay** 動 [pe] 支付；付款	**purchase** 動 [ˋpɝtʃəs] 購買

特價打折

auction 名 [ˋɔkʃən] 拍賣	**bargain** 動 [ˋbɑrgɪn] 討價還價	**closeout** 名 [ˋkloz͵aʊt] 清倉銷售
cut-rate 形 [ˋkʌt͵ret] 有打折的	**deal** 名 [dil] 交易；協議	**discount** 名 [ˋdɪskaʊnt] 折扣
dumping 名 [ˋdʌmpɪŋ] 抛售	**on sale** 片 拍賣中；出售的	**sale** 名 [sel] 拍賣；大減價

還有這些說法～
應急旅遊句會聽也會說

Is there any discount?
有沒有打折？

Do you have any Christmas promotions going on?
你們聖誕節有特惠活動嗎？

We're offering 20% off on all purchases over NT$3,000 today.
今天購物滿新台幣三千元可享八折優惠。

You can get a free gift with any purchase over NT$10,000.
只要購物超過新台幣一萬元，就會送您免費禮物。

It is on sale for up to 50% off.
最低可打到五折。

I am going to think about it. Thanks, though.
我要再考慮一下，還是謝謝你。

A **I'll take this one.**
我要買這個。

B **Do you need anything else?**
您還需要其他東西嗎？

How much are they? Is the price shown on the tag?
這些多少錢呢？是看標籤上面的價格嗎？

Are you ready to proceed to the checkout?
您要準備結帳了嗎？

Please pay at the checkout.
請到櫃檯結帳。

I'll take this to the checkout for you.
我先幫您拿到櫃檯。

Do you want to pay the bill now?
請問您要現在結帳嗎？

A Will that be all (for today)?
您還需要其他東西嗎？

B That's all for today./That's it. Thanks.
這樣就好了，謝謝。

A How much is the total after tax?
稅後是多少錢呢？

B That comes to $15./That's $15 altogether.
這樣總共十五元。

Your total is $85. Cash or credit card?
您購買的金額是八十五元，請問要用現金還是刷卡？

A You don't happen to have any change, do you?
您手邊剛好有零錢嗎？

B Sorry, I don't have any change.
不好意思，我沒有零錢。

Here's your change. Would you like a bag?
您的找零在這裡。您要袋子嗎？

Could I have a receipt, please?
麻煩給我收據，謝謝。

一定用得到～
3句話搞定旅遊大小事

121

詢問修改服務

It doesn't fit. Do you do alterations?
這件不太合身，你們可以修改嗎？

也能這樣說：

Can you alter the pants? Make them a little shorter, please.
你們可以修改褲長嗎？請幫我改短一點。

> **Sure, Madam. You have to pay for alterations, though.**
> 可以，小姐，但需要額外付費喔。

詢問可否退換

Can I return/exchange this if there is a problem?
有任何問題的話，都可以退貨／換貨嗎？

也能這樣說：

What is the return/exchange policy?
你們的退／換貨標準是什麼？

> **You can return it within 15 days if it has a defect.**
> 商品若有瑕疵，十五天以內都能退貨。

想要
退貨時

I'd like to return this.
我要退貨。

也能這樣說：

Can I return this T-shirt, please?
我可以退掉這件 T 恤嗎？

對方可能這樣回應

Do you have the receipt?
請問您有帶收據嗎？

旅途中也要會的單字　122

　退換貨政策

defect 名 [`dıfɛkt] 瑕疵；缺陷	**exchange** 名 [ıks`tʃendʒ] 換貨；交換	**faulty** 形 [`fɔltı] 有缺點的
quality 名 [`kwɑlətı] 品質	**refund** 動 [rı`fʌnd] 退款	**return** 動 [rı`tɜn] 退貨
subject to 片 依照…	**unused** 形 [ʌn`just] 未使用過的	**unwashed** 形 [ʌn`wɑʃt] 未洗過的

　修改服務

alter 動 [`ɔltɚ] 修改	**alteration** 名 [,ɔltə`reʃən] 修改（衣服）	**blind stitch** 片 藏針縫法
flat stitch 片 平針縫法	**hem** 名 [hɛm]（衣服的）摺邊	**seam** 名 [sim] 車縫處
stitch 名 [stıtʃ] 針法；針線	**take it in/out** 片 改緊 / 放寬	**take it up/down** 片 改長 / 改短

Could you make it knee-length?
可以把長度改到膝蓋嗎？

It's too loose. I'd like the waist altered to a smaller size.
穿起來太鬆了，腰圍麻煩改小一點。

A **How long will it take for the alterations?**
請問多久能改好呢？

B **You can get it back tomorrow.**
您明天就可以來拿了。

I bought this shirt here yesterday, but it's too small. Can I exchange it for a bigger one?
我昨天跟你們買了這件襯衫，但是太小了，可以換件大一點的嗎？

A **Alright, do you have the receipt?**
好的，您有帶收據嗎？

B **I have it right here.**
收據在這裡。

I'd like to change it for a larger size. Do you have these in extra large?
我想要換大一點的尺碼，你們有 XL 的嗎？

I found the quality was not what I had hoped for.
我發現商品品質跟我預期的不太一樣。

The sole is slippery, and I did not find them comfortable.

180

鞋底很滑，而且穿起來不怎麼舒適。

🔊 I want to return this pair of shoes.
我要退掉這雙鞋。

🔊 Can I get a new pair?
我可以換雙新的嗎？

🔊 We can repair the entire sole for you.
我們可以幫您把鞋底整個換掉。

A I need to return this cell phone that I just bought.
我想要退掉我剛買的手機。

B Is there a problem?
手機有什麼問題嗎？

🔊 Can I return it for a full refund if I don't like it?
如果我不喜歡這項產品，可以全額退費嗎？

🔊 Most items can be exchanged or refunded with a receipt within 30 days of purchase.
大部分的商品在購買三十天內，都可以持收據退換貨。

🔊 Not all products are returnable at the store.
不是所有的店內商品都可以退貨。

🔊 Things like movies, music and video games are not refundable.
像是電影光碟、唱片和電動遊戲都是不能退費的。

🔊 To get a full refund, items must be unworn and unwashed with all tags attached.
商品未穿過、洗過，且保留所有標籤，才能全額退費。

181

一定用得到～
3句話搞定旅遊大小事

說明目的時

I'd like to make a complaint, please.
我想要投訴。

也能這樣說：

I'd like to place a complaint about my holiday in Hawaii last week.
關於上週在夏威夷的假期，我想要投訴。

> **I'm sorry to hear that. What exactly was the problem?**
> 我很抱歉，請問您遇到什麼問題呢？

對方可能這樣回應

說明問題時

I'm sorry to bother you, but the soup has gone sour.
很抱歉打擾你，但湯好像壞掉了。

也能這樣說：

Excuse me. There's a funny taste with the soup.
不好意思，這道湯有怪味。

> **I am terribly sorry! I'll get you another one.**
> 真的很抱歉！我待會幫您換掉。

對方可能這樣回應

向經理反映

I want to see the manager.
請找你們的經理過來。

也能這樣說：

I'd like to speak to a manager, please.
麻煩找你們的經理過來。

I'm afraid he's not here at the moment.
很抱歉，我們經理目前不在。

對方可能這樣回應

 旅途中也要會的單字 125

表達不滿

complain 動 [kəm`plen] 投訴；抱怨	**complaint** 名 [kəm`plent] 投訴；抱怨	**dissatisfied** 形 [dɪs`sætɪs͵faɪd] 不滿的
feedback 名 [`fid͵bæk] 回饋	**insist** 動 [ɪn`sɪst] 堅持	**make a complaint** 片 投訴
manager 名 [`mænɪdʒɚ] 經理	**mistake** 名 [mɪ`stek] 過失；誤會	**report** 動 [rɪ`port] 描述；報告

服務態度

attitude 名 [`ætətjud] 態度	**compensation** 名 [͵kɑmpən`seʃən] 彌補；賠償	**customer service** 片 客戶服務
deal with sth. 片 處理某事	**difficult customer** 片 奧客	**guarantee** 名 動 [͵gærən`ti] 保證
resolve 動 [rɪ`zɑlv] 解決；解答	**request** 名 動 [rɪ`kwɛst] 要求；請求	**troubleshoot** 動 [`trʌbḷ͵ʃut] 分析並解決問題

183

A Excuse me. I would like to lodge a complaint.
不好意思，我想提出投訴。

B OK. What is it regarding?
好的，請問您遇到的問題是什麼呢？

Excuse me. I wonder if you can help me.
不好意思，可以幫我一個忙嗎？

What seems to be the problem?
請問您遇到什麼問題了呢？

Could you give me some details, please?
可以詳細說明一下您的問題嗎？

I'm sorry, but I'm not satisfied with this tour.
很抱歉這樣說，但我不怎麼滿意這次的旅行。

I am not happy at all with this service.
我非常不滿意這項服務。

A I am very dissatisfied with the service I received yesterday.
我非常不滿意你們昨天的服務。

B I'm sorry to hear that. Could you tell me what made you feel disappointed?
真的很抱歉。可以請您說明不滿意的原因嗎？

I'd like to know why the clerk pulled a long face at me.
我想知道為什麼店員擺臭臉給我看。

184

A I'd like an explanation for the mess in our room.
我想知道為什麼我們房間變得那麼亂。

B Please tell me exactly what happened.
麻煩您告訴我詳細的情形。

If you don't replace the product, I'll complain to the manager.
如果你不幫我更換產品的話，我就要向你們經理投訴。

I'm sorry, there's nothing I can do.
很抱歉，我無法幫您的忙。

I'm afraid it isn't our policy to give refunds, sir.
先生，這恐怕不適用我們的退款政策。

I'll check the details and get back to you later.
我會替您確認造成問題的原因，稍後與您聯繫。

OK. I'll look into it right away.
好的，我馬上替您查明原因。

Please, you're not listening to me at all!
拜託，你根本就沒有在聽我說話！

I'm sorry, but this is unacceptable!
不好意思，但這樣我完全不能接受！

I understand you're upset, sir.
先生，我知道您很生氣。

Is there anything else I need to know about this that I haven't thought to ask?
針對這個問題，請問您還有需要補充的嗎？

185

Part 5

嚐遍異地美食

Stimulating Your Taste Buds

It's a pity not to try out local foods!

身在國外，不嚐嚐道地美食就太可惜啦！

名 名詞　　動 動詞　　形 形容詞

副 副詞　　介 介係詞　　片 片語　　縮 縮寫

Eating Out At A Restaurant

預約餐廳與現場排隊

一定用得到～
3句話搞定旅遊大小事

127

詢問有無空位

Do you have a table for six?
你們有六個人的桌位嗎？

🔊 —也能這樣說：

May I make a reservation for six people tonight?
我想訂今晚六個人的位子。

> **Sorry. All the tables are reserved.**
> 很抱歉，所有的位子都被訂滿了。

對方可能這樣回應

預約桌位時

I'd like a table for two, please.
我想訂兩個人的位子。

🔊 —也能這樣說：

I would like to make a reservation for two for 6 o'clock.
我想預定六點鐘的兩個位子。

> **Sure. Please tell me your name and phone number.**
> 好的，請給我您的大名以及電話號碼。

對方可能這樣回應

選擇特定座位

Could we sit by the window, please?
我們可以坐窗邊的位子嗎？

 也能這樣說：

We'd like a table by the window, if possible.
如果窗邊還有位子的話，我們想坐窗邊。

 對方可能這樣回應

Yes, we do have a table available right now. Follow me, please.
好的，目前正好有空位，這邊請。

 旅途中也要會的單字 128

前往餐廳

book 動	cancel 動	dine 動
[buk] 預定；登記	[`kænsl] 取消；刪除	[daɪn] 進餐；用餐
dress code 片 服裝規定	**line up** 片 排隊	**make a reservation** 片 預約
postpone 動 [post`pon] 推遲；使延期	reserve 動 [rɪ`zɜv] 預約；保留	reservation 名 [ˌrɛzə`veʃən] 預定

餐廳座位

available 形 [ə`veləbḷ] 可用的；有空的	beforehand 副 [bɪ`for.hænd] 事先；預先	booth 名 [buθ] 雅座；攤販
high chair 片 高腳嬰兒椅	**in advance** 片 事先	party 名 [`partɪ] 一團人
private 形 [`praɪvɪt] 私人的	**private booth** 片 包廂	table 名 [`tebḷ] 桌子；一桌人

🔊 **Do I need to make a reservation in advance?**
我需要事先訂位嗎？

🔊 **The restaurant is usually busy. You'd better make a reservation first.**
這間餐廳總是一堆人，你最好先訂位。

🔊 **Sorry, we don't accept reservations on the phone on weekends.**
抱歉，我們週末都不接受電話訂位。

A **How many people are in your party, please?**
請問您們有多少人要用餐？
B **There are three of us.**
我們有三個人。

🔊 **Do you have a table free?**
你們還有空位嗎？

🔊 **We haven't booked a table. Can you fit us in?**
我們沒有訂位，請問現場還有位子嗎？

A **When will a table be available?**
幾點才會有位子呢？
B **We won't have a table open until 8 p.m.**
要到八點以後才會有空位喔。

🔊 **As soon as there are available seats, we will contact you immediately.**
一有空位我們就會馬上通知您。

190

We want a booth at 7:30 p.m., please.
我們要訂晚上七點半的包廂。

A How long will you hold a reservation?
訂位可以保留多久呢？

B The table will be held for ten minutes after your reservation time.
位子將會為您保留十分鐘。

I'd like to cancel my reservation for tomorrow.
我想取消明天的訂位。

I'd like to postpone my reservation for half an hour.
請將我的訂位延後半小時。

Is that table by the window reserved?
窗邊的那張桌子有人預約了嗎？

Would you prefer a smoking or non-smoking area?
請問您要坐吸煙區還是禁煙區？

Can we push these three tables together?
我們可以把這三張桌子併在一起嗎？

At what time do you serve dinner?
晚餐是從幾點開始供應呢？

How much longer do we have to wait?
我們還要等多久才會有位子呢？

We have a reservation for a table for two in the name of Smith.
我們有訂兩個位子，名字是史密斯。

Unit
02 Ordering Food In The Restaurant

在餐廳點餐

一定用得到～
3句話搞定旅遊大小事

130

想要
點餐時

I'm ready to order.
我想要點餐了。

🔊 也能這樣說：

I would like to order my food now, please.
麻煩現在幫我點餐，謝謝。

What would you like to order?
您要點什麼呢？

對方可能這樣回應

點菜
這樣說

I'd like a Caesar salad.
請給我一份凱薩沙拉。

🔊 也能這樣說：

I'd like to start with an appetizer.
我想先點個開胃菜。

Sure. Anything else?
沒問題，還要什麼呢？

對方可能這樣回應

192

問菜是什麼

What's a 'black pudding'?
請問「黑布丁」是什麼？

🔊 也能這樣說：

What's in the 'black pudding'?
「黑布丁」裡面有加什麼呢？

> **It is made from pork fat and pork blood.**
> 它主要是由豬油和豬血製成的。

對方可能這樣回應

 旅途中也要會的單字 131

📍 點餐時間

menu 名 [`mɛnju] 菜單	**order** 名 動 [`ɔrdɚ] 點餐	**platter** 名 [`plætɚ] 一大盤
recommend 動 [ˌrɛkə`mɛnd] 推薦；建議	**server** 名 [`sɝvɚ] 服務生	**starving** 形 [`starvɪŋ] 飢餓的
take sb.'s order 片 幫某人點餐	**waiter** 名 [`wetɚ] 男服務生	**waitress** 名 [`wetrɪs] 女服務生

📍 正式西餐

aperitif 名 [ɑperɪ`tif] 餐前酒	**appetizer** 名 [`æpəˌtaɪzɚ] 開胃菜	**dessert** 名 [dɪ`zɝt] 甜點
entrée 名 [`antre] 主菜	**main course** 片 主菜	**starter** 名 [`startɚ] 開胃菜
utensil 名 [ju`tɛnsḷ] 餐具	**vegan** 名 [`vɛɡən] 素食主義者	**wine list** 片 酒單

I'll take your order in a few minutes.
我等一下再過來幫您點餐。

May I bring you something to drink?
您要先喝點飲料嗎？

May I have a look at the wine list?
我可以看一下酒單嗎？

Do you have a menu in Chinese?
你們餐廳有中文菜單嗎？

Would you like to order now?/Are you ready to order?
您要點餐了嗎？

What can I get for you?
您要點什麼呢？

Ⓐ What is the soup of the day?
本日推薦湯品是什麼湯呢？

Ⓑ We have onion soup and borsch.
我們今天有洋蔥湯和羅宋湯。

Ⓐ How large are the portions?
這是幾人份的呢？

Ⓑ It's for four to six people.
夠四個人到六個人吃。

Have you decided on your entrée?

194

您決定好要點什麼主菜了嗎？

A **Would you like some soup?**
您要點湯嗎？

B **I'll have the corn soup with puff pastry.**
我要酥皮玉米濃湯。

A **How would you like your steak done?**
您的牛排要幾分熟？

B **I want it medium well, please.**
我要七分熟。

I don't want it too spicy.
我的餐點不要太辣。

I'll have the same dish as that gentleman.
我想要點和那位先生一樣的菜。

A **Would you like to order anything else, sir?**
先生，您還要點其他菜嗎？

B **No, that will be all. Thanks.**
不用了，謝謝，這些就夠了。

A **Would you like your tea with your dinner or later?**
請問您的茶要跟晚餐一起上，還是餐後再上？

B **With my dinner, please.**
跟晚餐一起，謝謝。

Let me repeat your order.
我重複一下您的餐點。

Your order will be ready soon.
餐點稍後就會為您送上。

Unit 03 Savoring Delicious Specialties
品嘗美味菜餚

一定用得到～
3句話搞定旅遊大小事

詢問今日特餐

What's today's special?
今天的特餐是什麼呢？

也能這樣說：

What is the house special today?
請問今日特餐是什麼？

> The Alaska salmon is today's special.
> 今日特餐是阿拉斯加鮭魚。

對方可能這樣回應

請服務生推薦

What do you recommend?
你推薦什麼菜呢？

也能這樣說：

This is my first time here. Could you recommend something special?
這是我第一次來，你可以推薦一些特別的菜嗎？

> You can try our pig knuckle with sauerkraut or sausage.
> 你可以試試我們的德國豬腳加酸菜，或來份香腸。

對方可能這樣回應

詢問
招牌菜

What's your specialty?
你們的招牌菜是什麼呢？

也能這樣說：

What's the specialty of your restaurant?
你們餐廳的招牌菜是什麼呢？

對方可能這樣回答

Our salami spaghetti is very good.
我們的臘腸義大利麵很好吃喔。

旅途中也要會的單字　134

當季美味

delicate 形	delicious 形	flavorful 形
[`dɛləkɪt] 精緻的；鮮美的	[dɪ`lɪʃəs] 美味的；可口的	[`flevəfəl] 有風味的
in season 片 當季的	**rich** 形 [rɪtʃ]（食物）味濃的	**special** 名 [`spɛʃəl] 特餐
tasty 形 [`testɪ] 美味的	**tender** 形 [`tɛndə] 軟嫩的	**tuck into** 片 狼吞虎嚥

品味牛排

medium rare 片 三分熟的	medium 形 [`midɪəm] 五分熟的	medium well 片 七分熟的
prime rib 片 牛前胸的上等肋條	**rare** 形 [rɛr] 一分熟的	**steak** 名 [stek] 牛排
sirloin 名 [`sɝlɔɪn] 沙朗（牛腰上方的肉）	**tenderloin** 名 [`tɛndə,lɔɪn]（牛、豬的）里脊肉	**well-done** 形 [`wɛl`dʌn] 全熟的

135

Ⓐ I'll try the lobster.
我想吃吃看龍蝦。

Ⓑ Good choice! It's our most popular dish!
選得真好！那是我們最受歡迎的菜呢！

📢 **What's in season right now?**
現在當季的食材有什麼呢？

📢 **May I suggest our specialty—shish kebabs?**
您可以嚐嚐我們的招牌肉串。

📢 **Our roast beef is a best-seller.**
我們的烤牛肉是最受歡迎的。

📢 **Many guests like our smoked salmon.**
很多客人都喜歡我們的煙燻鮭魚。

📢 **I'd like some German beer to go with the pig knuckle.**
我想要點個德國啤酒來配豬腳。

📢 **Is there any particular brand of beer you like?**
您有特別想要點哪一牌的啤酒嗎？

📢 **Our salmon is very fresh, and it comes with a glass of white wine.**
我們的鮭魚非常新鮮，而且點鮭魚還送一杯白酒。

📢 **I'd like to try some Mexican food.**
我想吃點墨西哥菜。

Our fried turnip cake with XO sauce is very popular.
我們的 XO 醬炒蘿蔔糕很受歡迎喔。

Barbecued pork buns are our top dish.
蜜汁叉燒包是我們這邊最受客人歡迎的菜。

Your lasagna, sir.
先生，您點的千層麵來了。

Thanks. It looks great.
謝謝，看起來很好吃。

Excuse me. Could we have some more water?
不好意思，可以幫我們加點水嗎？

Excuse me. Is everything all right?
不好意思打擾了，用餐都還好嗎？

The steak is very tender and juicy. I love it.
牛排又軟又多汁，我很喜歡。

How are your pork chops?
你點的豬排好吃嗎？

Their sashimi is very fresh and flavorful.
他們的生魚片很新鮮也很美味。

I've never had such a delicious roast beef before!
我從來沒吃過這麼好吃的烤牛肉！

The fries are crispy. Yummy!
薯條很脆，很好吃！

Unit 04 Complaints & Suggestions

向餐廳提出建議

一定用得到～
3句話搞定旅遊大小事

送錯餐點時

I'm sorry, but I didn't order this.
不好意思，我沒有點這個。

 — 也能這樣說：

I'm sorry, but this isn't what I ordered.
不好意思，我點的不是這道菜。

對方可能這樣回應

May I ask what you ordered again?
可以再請問一次您點了什麼嗎？

拿到冷掉的菜

These noodles are cold. Can you bring me another dish?
這碗麵冷掉了，可以給我另一碗嗎？

 — 也能這樣說：

Sorry, but my food is cold. Could you warm it up for me, please?
不好意思，我的食物冷掉了。可以幫我加熱嗎？

對方可能這樣回應

I'll bring you another one.
我再換一份餐點給您。

久久不見餐點

Any idea how much longer it will be?
還要多久才會上菜呢？

也能這樣說：

Could you check on our order?
你能催一下我們的餐點嗎？

I'll check with the chef and see if he can speed up your orders.
我跟主廚確定一下，看他可不可以快點幫你們煮好。

對方可能這樣回應

旅途中也要會的單字

137

 口味不合

bitter 形 [`bɪtɚ] 苦的	**greasy** 形 [`grizɪ] 油膩的	**musty** 形 [`mʌstɪ] 發霉的
spicy 形 [`spaɪsɪ] 辣的	**stale** 形 [stel] 不新鮮的	**strange** 形 [strendʒ] 奇怪的
tasteless 形 [`testlɪs] 沒味道的	**unseasoned** 形 [ʌn`siznd] 未加調味料的	**weird** 形 [wɪrd] 奇怪的

 提出建議

advice 名 [əd`vaɪs] 建議；指點	**cater** 動 [`ketɚ] 提供飲食；迎合	**chef** 名 [ʃɛf] 主廚
comment 名 [`kɑmɛnt] 意見	**comment card** 片 留言卡	**criticize** 動 [`krɪtɪ͵saɪz] 批評；評論
foodie 名 [`fudɪ] （俚）美食家	**gourmet** 名 [`gʊrme] 美食家	**suggest** 動 [sə`dʒɛst] 提議；建議

A I've been waiting for 20 minutes for my order.
我已經等了二十分鐘，餐點怎麼都還沒來。

B I'm sorry, but Saturday night is our busiest night of the week.
很抱歉，星期六剛好是我們最忙的時候。

The chicken is tasteless.
雞肉一點味道都沒有。

The fried rice is too salty and too greasy.
炒飯太鹹也太油了。

This steak is undercooked! It's almost raw!
這塊牛排沒有熟！根本就是生的吧！

A Didn't you order your steak rare?
您不是點一分熟的牛排嗎？

B No, I ordered it well-done.
不是，我點的是全熟。

My steak is too tough. I think it was overcooked.
我的牛排太老了，可能是煮太久了。

The seafood is not fresh. It tastes sour.
海鮮不新鮮，味道有點酸掉了。

Excuse me, but this soup is too spicy.
不好意思，這湯太辣了。

I'm sorry about the mistake.

非常抱歉，我們弄錯您的餐點了。

Some flies are flying around my food. I can't eat it.
一堆蒼蠅在我旁邊飛來飛去，這樣我沒辦法好好吃飯。

A **My spoon is dirty.**
我的湯匙是髒的。

B **I'm very sorry, sir. I'll get you a new one immediately.**
很抱歉，先生，我幫您拿新的湯匙過來。

Sorry, but I think I got the wrong order.
不好意思，菜好像上錯了。

This isn't what I was expecting at all. Could I try something else?
這跟我期待的差太多了吧，我可以換成別道菜嗎？

A **I don't want to make a scene, but there's a fly in my soup.**
我不想大驚小怪，但我的湯裡面有隻蒼蠅。

B **I am terribly sorry! I will take the soup back to the kitchen and get you another one.**
非常抱歉！我去廚房幫您換一碗湯過來。

Is this the teriyaki chicken set that I ordered?
這是我點的照燒雞肉嗎？

A **I'm sorry that my son spilled the juice all over the table.**
不好意思，我兒子打翻果汁，弄得整張桌子都是。

B **No worries. I'll clean up your table right away.**
沒關係，我馬上幫您清理桌子。

Finishing Your Meal & Paying The Bill

拍拍肚皮結帳去

一定用得到～
3句話搞定旅遊大小事

想要打包時

Please wrap this up for me.
麻煩幫我打包。

（也能這樣說：）

Could you give me a doggie bag, please?
可以給我一個打包的袋子嗎？

> **Sure. Just a minute, please.**
> 好的，請稍等。

對方可能這樣回應

想要結帳時

Check, please.
麻煩幫我結帳。

（也能這樣說：）

Could I have the bill, please?
麻煩幫我買單，謝謝。

> **OK. I'll bring your check in a minute.**
> 好的，我待會就把帳單拿給您。

對方可能這樣回應

想要分
開付錢

We'd like to pay separately, please.
我們想分開付錢。

也能這樣說：

Can we get separate bills?
我們可以分開結帳嗎？

Sure. Set A is $15, and Set B is $13.
沒問題，A 套餐是十五元，B 套餐是十三元。

對方可能這樣回應

旅途中也要會的單字 140

用餐完畢

carton 名 [`kɑrtn̩] 紙盒	**complimentary** 形 [ˌkɑnpləˋmɛntərɪ] 贈送的	**customer service** 片 顧客服務
doggie bag 片 打包袋	**free of charge** 片 免費的	**leftover** 名 [`lɛft͵ovɚ] 剩飯 / 菜
on the house 片（店家）請客	**regular** 名 [`rɛgjələ] 常客	**wrap up** 片 包好；打包

餐廳結帳

amount 名 [əˋmaunt] 總額；總數	**bill** 名 [bɪl] 帳單	**charge** 名 [tʃɑrdʒ] 費用
check 名 [tʃɛk] 帳單	**gratuity** 名 [grəˋtjuətɪ] 小費	**overcharge** 動 [`ovɚˋtʃɑrdʒ] 索價過高
pay the bill 片 付款	**separate** 形 [`sɛpə͵ret] 分開的	**split** 動 [splɪt] 分開；分擔

還有這些說法～
應急旅遊句會聽也會說

Could we get the bill, please?
麻煩幫我們買單，謝謝。

A Unfortunately, we have to head to the theater, so could we pay now?
我們得趕去劇場了，可以現在結帳嗎？

B Certainly, sir. I'll bring you the bill.
當然可以，先生。我待會把您的帳單拿過來。

You can take the rest of your chicken home in a doggie bag.
你可以把剩下的雞肉打包回家。

Would you like me to wrap this up for you?
要幫您打包嗎？

Can you give me a to-go box?
可以給我一個外帶的盒子嗎？

How much is the total?
總共多少錢呢？

It's on me./I'll pay the bill./It's my treat.
這餐我請客。

Let's go Dutch./Let's split it.
我們各付各的吧。

Would you like me to split your check?
您們的帳單要分開結嗎？

A Should I leave the money with you?
錢給你就可以了嗎？

B No. Please pay at the cash register.
不是，請到櫃檯結帳。

Does the price include the service charge?/Is service included?
價錢有包含服務費嗎？

A How much tip should we leave?
我們該給多少小費呢？

B People usually leave 15 percent of the bill to the server.
大家通常都會留帳單總價的百分之十五做為小費。

Can I pay by credit card?
可以用信用卡嗎？

Could you check the bill for me, please? It doesn't seem right.
可以幫我確認一下金額嗎？帳單好像算錯了。

I think you may have made a mistake with the bill.
你們帳單上的價錢好像算錯了。

A Was everything to your satisfaction?
您還滿意今天的餐點嗎？

B The whole meal was delicious! Our compliments to the chef.
每道菜都很好吃！請向主廚表達我們的謝意。

06 Dining At A Fast-Food Restaurant

在速食店用餐

一定用得到～
3句話搞定旅遊大小事

142

點套餐時
Combo number 3, please.
請給我三號餐。

 也能這樣說：

I'll take a Combo number 3.
我想點三號餐。

> **Would you like to go large?**
> 請問附餐要加大嗎？

對方可能這樣回答

單點點餐時
I'd like a double cheeseburger, please.
請給我一個雙層起司漢堡。

 也能這樣說：

May I have a double cheeseburger?
可以給我一個雙層起司漢堡嗎？

> **Would you like everything on it?**
> 配料全部都要加嗎？

對方可能這樣回答

問可否
加料

Can I have extra cheese?
可以多加一些起司嗎？

也能這樣說：

May I have more cheese, please?
可以多加一些起司嗎？

對方可能這樣回答

Of course. That'll be $12.5 in total.
當然可以，您的餐點總共是十二塊五。

旅途中也要會的單字 **143**

 速食餐廳

dine in/for here 片 在店內用餐；內用	**drive-through** 名 [`draɪvˌθru] 得來速	**fast food** 片 速食
jumbo 形 [`dʒʌmbo] 特大的	**lid** 名 [lɪd] 蓋子	**plastic utensil** 片 塑膠餐具
refill 名 [`rifɪl]（飲料）續杯	**takeout** 名 [`tekˌaʊt] 外帶餐點	**to go** 片 外帶

 速食餐點

burger 名 [`bɝgɚ] 漢堡	**calorie** 名 [`kælərɪ] 熱量	**cheeseburger** 名 [`tʃizˌbɝgɚ] 起司漢堡
chicken nugget 片 雞塊	**Coke** 名 [kok] 可樂	**combo** 名 [`kɑmbo] 套餐；組合餐
French fries 片 薯條	**milkshake** 名 [ˌmɪlk`ʃek] 奶昔	**set** 名 [sɛt] 套餐

144

🔊 **May I take your order?/What can I get for you today?**
您要點什麼呢？

🔊 **Two hamburgers and two coffees to go, please.**
我要外帶兩份漢堡和兩杯咖啡。

🔊 **I'd like a filet-o-fish, with a medium Coke, please.**
我要一個麥香魚漢堡，加中杯可樂，謝謝。

🔊 **I'd like a Big Mac with extra cheese.**
我要一份大麥克漢堡，要多加起司。

Ⓐ **I'd like to order a chicken burger and a large order of French fries.**
我要一個雞肉漢堡和大份的薯條。

Ⓑ **Is that for here or for takeout?**
內用還是帶走？

🔊 **One beef burger and an orange juice, please.**
請給我一份牛肉漢堡和一杯柳橙汁。

🔊 **I 'll have a number six—the large hamburger, large fries, and iced tea.**
我想點六號餐，漢堡和薯條要加大，飲料要冰茶。

Ⓐ **What do you want on your burger?**
請問您的漢堡上面要加什麼？

Ⓑ **I'll have lettuce, cucumber, olives, and red onion.**
我要加生菜、小黃瓜、黑橄欖和紫洋蔥。

A Would you like anything to drink?
您要飲料嗎？

B Coke, please.
我要可樂，謝謝。

A Would you like a large Coke for 50 cents more?
您要加大可樂嗎？只要多付五十分美元喔。

B No, thanks.
不用了，謝謝。

🔊 Is the Coke large or small?
可樂要大杯還是小杯的？

🔊 Where can I get a straw and napkins?
請問哪裡有吸管和餐巾紙？

🔊 Do you charge for refills?
飲料續杯要收費嗎？

A Would you like fries with that?
您想要加薯條嗎？

B Large curly fries, please.
我要大的波浪薯條，謝謝。

A Which sauce do you like?
您要哪種醬料呢？

B Ketchup/BBQ sauce/sweet'n'sour sauce, please.
我要番茄醬 / BBQ 燒烤醬 / 糖醋醬，謝謝。

A Is that it?/Will that be all?
還要點其他的嗎？

B Yes, that's it.
這樣就好了。

一定用得到～
3句話搞定旅遊大小事

點咖啡這樣說

I'll have an Americano, please.
請給我一杯美式咖啡。

🔊 也能這樣說：

Can I get a tall, hot coffee?
可以給我一杯大杯的熱咖啡嗎？

對方可能這樣回應

Would you like sugar or cream in it?
您要加糖或奶精嗎？

請再來一杯

Could I have some more coffee, please?
請再給我一些咖啡，好嗎？

🔊 也能這樣說：

May I have another cup of coffee?
可以再給我一杯咖啡嗎？

對方可能這樣回應

Sure. I'll bring your coffee in a minute.
當然可以，我等等幫您拿過來。

臨時加點配料

Could I have some honey with my pancakes?
可以加點蜂蜜來配我的鬆餅嗎？

也能這樣說：

Could you add some honey to the pancakes I ordered?
可以加點蜂蜜到我剛剛點的鬆餅上面嗎？

對方可能這樣回應

No problem. Extra honey will cost you 50 cents, though.
沒有問題，但多加蜂蜜要多付五十分喔。

旅途中也要會的單字 146

西式早餐

bagel 名 [`beɡəl] 貝果	**muffin** 名 [`mʌfɪn] 鬆餅	**omelet** 名 [`ɑmlɪt] 煎蛋捲
pancake 名 [`pæn͵kek] 鬆餅；薄煎餅	**pie** 名 [paɪ] 派；餡餅	**scone** 名 [skon] （英）司康餅
tart 名 [tɑrt] 水果餡餅；甜塔	**toast** 名 [tost] 吐司	**wholegrain** 形 [`holɡren] 全麥的

香醇咖啡

Americano 名 [ə͵mɛrɪ`kano] 美式咖啡	**cappuccino** 名 [͵kɑpə`tʃino] 卡布奇諾	**espresso** 名 [ɛs`prɛso] 義式濃縮咖啡
house blend 片 特調咖啡	**latte** 名 [`læte] 拿鐵	**milk foam** 片 奶泡
mocha 名 [`mokə] 摩卡	**ounce (oz.)** 名 [auns] 盎司	**whipped cream** 片 鮮奶油

🔊 **This is our breakfast menu.**
這是我們早餐的菜單。

🔊 **What do you feel like eating this morning?**
您今天早上想吃什麼？

🔊 **Today's special is ham and eggs. You can choose toast or cereal, and orange juice or grapefruit juice.**
今日特餐是火腿蛋，您可以選擇搭配吐司或燕麥粥，飲料可以選柳橙汁或葡萄柚汁。

🔊 **May I order takeout here?**
我可以點外帶嗎？

🅐 **We have two set meals for breakfast: continental and American breakfast.**
我們的早餐套餐有兩種選擇——歐式和美式早餐。

🅑 **What's the difference between these two?**
這兩種套餐有什麼不同呢？

🔊 **Could I get some cinnamon rolls and a flat white?**
麻煩給我肉桂捲和一杯白咖啡。

🔊 **We'd like to try a fruit tart and a crème brulee.**
我們想吃吃看水果塔和烤布蕾。

🔊 **We serve two kinds of jam—blueberry and strawberry. Which do you prefer?**
我們提供兩種果醬，有藍莓醬和草莓醬，您要哪種呢？

Do you want some maple syrup to go with the pancakes?
您的鬆餅要不要配點楓糖漿？

A **How do you like your eggs? Scrambled or boiled?**
您的蛋要炒蛋還是水煮蛋？

B **Soft-boiled, please.**
請給我糖心蛋。

I'd like my eggs sunny-side-up.
我想要太陽蛋。

I want my eggs over hard.
我的蛋兩面都要熟的。

I'll have a pot of Earl tea and a slice of apple pie.
我想要點一壺伯爵茶和一片蘋果派。

Could I have herbal tea instead of oolong tea?
我可以把烏龍茶換成花草茶嗎？

I'd like my coffee without cream.
我的咖啡不要加奶精。

I'll take a sandwich with extra bacon.
我想點一份三明治，要多加一些培根。

A **Would you like whipped cream with your pie?**
您的派上面要加鮮奶油嗎？

B **No, thank you. Could I have ice cream with it instead?**
不用，謝謝。可以改加冰淇淋嗎？

入住當地旅館

Satisfying Accommodations

*Choosing the right accommodation
can sometimes be a little bit tricky!*

住宿選擇百百種，當然要選個舒適的好地方住！

名 名詞 　動 動詞 　形 形容詞

副 副詞 　介 介係詞 　片 片語 　縮 縮寫

Looking For Accommodations

臨時找住宿

一定用得到～
3句話搞定旅遊大小事

詢問有無空房

Do you have any rooms available?
你們還有空房嗎？

也能這樣說：

Is there any vacancy?
請問還有空房嗎？

I'm sorry, but we are fully booked.
很抱歉，房間都被訂滿了。

詢問住宿價格

What's the rate for the room?
這間房間一晚多少錢呢？

也能這樣說：

How much is it per night?
一個晚上多少錢呢？

Your room is two hundred and ninety dollars per night.
您的房間一個晚上是兩百九十元。

What's included in this cost?
這個價錢有包含什麼呢？

也能這樣說：

What do you include in the room rate?
房價有包含什麼呢？

A full continental buffet every morning is included.
有附每天的全套歐陸自助式早餐。

旅途中也要會的單字 149

 房源選擇

bed & breakfast (B&B) 片 民宿	**capsule hotel** 片 膠囊旅館	**guesthouse** 名 [`gɛst.haʊs] 家庭旅館
hostel 名 [`hɑstl̩] 旅社	**hotel** 名 [ho`tɛl] 旅館；飯店	**inn** 名 [ɪn] 小旅館；客棧
lodge 名 [lɑdʒ] 小木屋；山林小屋	**resort** 名 [rɪ`zɔrt] 度假村；名勝	**youth hostel** 片 青年旅館

 預約須知

backpacker 名 [`bæk.pækɚ] 背包客	**booking** 名 [`bʊkɪŋ] 預定；預約	**cancellation policy** 片 取消訂房的規定
charge 動 [tʃɑrdʒ] 索價	**cost** 名動 [kɔst] 花費	**fully** 副 [`fʊlɪ] 完全地；充分地
per 介 [pɚ] 每；每一	**rate** 名 [ret] 費用；價格	**vacancy** 名 [`vekənsɪ] 空房；空處

When you travel to popular destinations during peak seasons, you'd better reserve accommodations before the trip.
當你在旺季去熱門景點旅遊時，最好在出發前先預訂好房間。

I am looking for a hotel under NT$2,000.
我在找台幣兩千元以下的旅館。

What's not included in this price?
這個價格沒有包含什麼呢？

A Good morning, Luxury Hotel. How may I help you?
早安，這裡是極致奢華飯店，我能夠為您服務嗎？

B Hello, I'd like to make a reservation.
你好，我想要訂房。

Hold on, please. I'll put you through to the reservation center.
請稍後，我幫您轉接到訂房中心。

A When will that be for?
請問您要預約什麼時候的房間？

B I will be arriving on the first of January.
我會在一月一日入住。

I'm sorry, but we are fully booked.
很抱歉，我們已經客滿了。

Could you recommend another hotel?
你能介紹別家旅館嗎？

I'd like to book a room for next weekend. What are your rates?
我想要訂下週末的一間房間，請問房價是多少？

Ⓐ How many nights will you be staying?
請問您要住幾個晚上？

Ⓑ I'll be staying for five nights.
我要住五個晚上。

Ⓐ How many people is the reservation for?
請問有幾位要入住？

Ⓑ There will be two of us.
我們有兩個人。

Ⓐ What name will the reservation be listed under?
請問您的貴姓大名？

Ⓑ Charles Hannighan.
我叫查爾斯・漢尼根。

Ⓐ Could you spell your last name for me, please?
可以請您拼一下您的姓氏嗎？

Ⓑ Sure. H-A-N-N-I-G-H-A-N.
好，是 HANNIGHAN。

Ⓐ Is there a phone number where you can be contacted?
請問您的聯絡電話是幾號？

Ⓑ Yes, my cell phone number is 485-174-6869.
我的手機號碼是 485-174-6869。

Do you have any branches in Europe?
你們飯店有歐洲分店嗎？

Booking Accommodations In Advance

事先預訂理想住宿

一定用得到～
3句話搞定旅遊大小事

預約
房間

We would like a room with two double beds.
我們想要訂有兩張雙人床的房間。

🔊 也能這樣說：

Please give us a room with two double beds.
請給我們有兩張雙人床的房間。

對方可能這樣回應

May I have your name, please?
請問您的貴姓大名？

增加
人數時

Can we add an extra bed?
我們可以再多加一張床嗎？

🔊 也能這樣說：

Is it possible to add one more person to our reservation?
我們的入住人數可以再多加一個人嗎？

對方可能這樣回應

Sure, but an extra bed will cost you $15 per night.
當然可以，但加床的話每晚會多收十五元喔。

確認預定資訊

Could you please check for my reservation?
可以幫我確認一下訂房嗎？

◀ **也能這樣說：**

I'd like to confirm my reservation, please.
我想要確認一下我的訂房，謝謝。

Certainly. What's the name your reservation is under?
好的，請問您是用哪個名字訂房的呢？

對方可能這樣回應

 旅途中也要會的單字 152

各種房型

double room 片 雙人房	**studio** 名 [`stjudɪ, o] 套房	**junior suite** 片 精緻套房
presidential suite 片 總統套房	**quadruple room** 片 四人房	**single room** 片 單人房
suite 名 [swit] 套房	**twin room** 片 雙床房	**villa** 名 [`vɪlə] 別墅套房

房間要求

adjoining room 片 相鄰房	**connecting room** 片 連通房	**deluxe** 形 [dɪ`lʌks] 豪華的
double bed 片 雙人床	**king-size bed** 片 加大雙人床	**queen-size bed** 片 加大雙人床
standard 形 [`stændəd] 標準的	**rollaway bed** 片 折疊床	**triple** 形 [`trɪpl̩] 三人的

🔊 **Have you stayed with us before?**
您以前有住過我們飯店嗎？

Ⓐ **What kind of room would you like to book?**
請問您要訂哪種房間？

Ⓑ **I'd like to reserve a double room.**
我要訂一間雙人房。

🔊 **What kind of room would you prefer?**
請問您比較喜歡什麼樣的房間？

🔊 **I'd like a room with a view, if possible.**
可能的話，我想要有風景可以看的房間。

🔊 **I prefer a room with an ocean view.**
我想要一間有海景的房間。

🔊 **We'd like to have a quiet, non-smoking room with a mountain view.**
我們想要訂個安靜又有山景的禁煙房。

🔊 **Would you like a king-size bed or a twin-bedded room?**
您要一張大床還是兩張小床？

🔊 **How much are your rooms?**
請問你們的房價是多少？

🔊 **What's the room rate for your water villa?**
你們的水上屋要多少錢？

A How much is it for a standard room?
一間標準客房多少錢？

B Our rates for single rooms are NT$2,000, and doubles are NT$2,500.
我們的單人房每晚新台幣兩千元，雙人房則是兩千五百元。

A How about a suite?
套房要多少錢？

B Suites are $3,600 per night.
套房是每晚三千六百元。

A Does the price include tax?
請問價錢有含稅嗎？

B The service charge and tax are included.
價錢包括服務費和稅金。

A Do you have any discount if we stay longer?
我們如果住久一點，房價會打折嗎？

B Yes, we offer a 15% discount if you stay for six days and over.
有的，住六晚以上房價會打八五折。

A What kind of room do you need? A smoking or non-smoking room?
請問您要吸煙還是禁煙的房間？

B I'd like a non-smoking room.
請給我禁煙房。

📢 Is there anything else I can assist you with?
還有什麼需要協助的嗎？

225

一定用得到～
3句話搞定旅遊大小事

辦理入住時

I'd like to check in, please.
我想要辦理入住。

也能這樣說：

Can I check in now, please?
現在可以辦理入住嗎？

對方可能這樣回應

May I have your ID or passport, please?
麻煩給我您的身分證或護照。

已有預定房間

I have a reservation under the name of Chris Tailor.
我有預定房間，名字是克里斯·泰勒。

也能這樣說：

I reserved a room through Booking.com. My name is Chris Tailor.
我有用 Booking.com 預定房間，名字是克里斯·泰勒。

對方可能這樣回應

Yes, a single business suite for two nights.
有的，是兩晚的單人商務套房。

226

Does the charge include breakfast?
費用有包含早餐嗎？

也能這樣說：

Is breakfast included in the room rate?
費用有包含早餐嗎？

Yes, a complimentary breakfast buffet is offered every morning.
有的，您每天早上都可以享用自助式早餐。

 旅途中也要會的單字 155

基本設施

business center	elevator 名	fitness center
片 商務中心	[`ɛlə,vetɚ]（美）電梯	片 健身中心
front desk	**lift** 名	**lobby** 名
片 服務檯	[lɪft]（英）電梯	[`labɪ] 大廳
luggage storage	**parking lot**	**reception** 名
片 寄放行李處	片 停車場	[rɪ`sɛpʃən] 服務檯

服務人員

bellboy 名	concierge 名	doorman 名
[`bɛl,bɔɪ]	[,kansɪ`ɛrʒ] 門房；禮賓	[`dor,mæn] 禮賓司
提行李的服務生		
housekeeping 名	**operator** 名	**porter** 名
[`haus,kipɪŋ] 房務	[`apə,retɚ] 接線員	[`portɚ] 提行李的服務生
receptionist 名	**uniform** 名	**valet** 名
[rɪ`sɛpʃənɪst] 接待員	[`junə,fɔrm] 制服	[`væle] 泊車服務員

A Do you have a reservation?
請問您有訂房嗎？

B Yes, but I forgot my hotel confirmation number.
我有訂房，但我忘了我的預約確認號碼了。

A moment, please. I'll look for your reservation details.
請稍後，我查一下您的訂房資料。

Yes, Mr. Chang. Your room is ready.
有的，張先生，您的房間已經準備好了。

Please fill out the registration card with your name and address.
請在住宿登記卡上面寫上您的姓名和住址。

Your room is 513. Here are the key cards.
您的房間在 513，這是您的房卡。

A I need an extra bed. How much should I pay?
我需要加一張床，請問要付多少錢？

B You have to pay NT$600 for an extra bed.
加一張床的費用是新台幣六百元。

Would you like the continental breakfast or the American breakfast?
您想要歐式早餐還是美式早餐？

Breakfast is provided from 6:30 to 10 o'clock every morning.

每天早上六點半到十點會提供早餐。

To guarantee your hotel reservation, it is necessary to pay for the first night as a deposit.
為了幫您保留房間，您必須先付第一晚的費用當作押金。

A Is the deposit refundable?
押金是可以退還的嗎？

B Yes, it will be refunded after your stay.
是的，在您退房之後會退還給您。

A How much notice do you require for a reservation cancellation?
取消訂房要多久前通知你們飯店呢？

B We require a 48-hour notice.
四十八小時之前必須通知我們。

How far are you from the airport?
你們飯店離機場多遠？

A Do you provide shuttles to and from the airport?
你們飯店有提供機場來回接送嗎？

B Yes. We have a free shuttle bus service.
有的，我們有提供免費的機場接駁。

A Do you need any help with your luggage?
您需要幫忙提行李嗎？

B No, thank you. I can carry them myself.
不用了，謝謝。我可以自己拿。

We provide a newspaper every morning. What newspaper would you like?
我們每天早上都有提供報紙，您想要看哪家報紙呢？

一定用得到～
3句話搞定旅遊大小事

157

使用內線點餐

This is room 262. I'd like to order some sandwiches.
這是 262 號房，我想點三明治。

 ─ 也能這樣說：

Could you send room 262 some sandwiches, please?
可以麻煩你送三明治到 262 號房嗎？

Of course. We'll send it up to your room in 15 minutes.
沒問題，我們十五分鐘內會送去您的房間。

對方可能這樣回應

索取物品

Can we have one more toiletry kit?
我們可以多要一組盥洗用品嗎？

 ─ 也能這樣說：

I'd like to request one more toiletry kit, please.
我想要多一組盥洗用品，謝謝。

Sure. Someone will be up with your kit shortly.
好的，我們等等會派人把您要的用品送上去。

對方可能這樣回應

230

要求叫醒服務

I need a wake-up call tomorrow morning.
我明天早上需要電話叫醒服務。

也能這樣說：

Can you give me a wake-up call tomorrow morning?
明天早上可以用電話叫我起床嗎？

Of course. When would you like the call?
當然可以，什麼時候叫您起床呢？

對方可能這樣回應

旅途中也要會的單字　158

 專人服務

amenity 名 [əˋmɪnətɪ] 便利設施	**babysit** 動 [ˋbebɪ͵sɪt] 替人看管嬰兒	**bicycle rental** 片 腳踏車租借
dry cleaning 片 乾洗	**laundry** 名 [ˋlɔndrɪ] 送洗衣物	**pantry** 名 [ˋpæntrɪ] 食品儲藏室
room attendant 片 客房服務員	**room service** 片 客房服務	**wake-up call** 片 電話叫醒服務

 客房設施

air conditioner 片 冷氣；空調	**cable TV** 片 有線電視	**coffee maker** 片 咖啡機
hairdryer 名 [ˋhɛr͵draɪɚ] 吹風機	**iron** 動 [ˋaɪən] 熨衣；燙平	**Jacuzzi** 名 [dʒəˋkuzɪ] 按摩浴缸
kitchenette 名 [͵kɪtʃɪnˋɛt] 小廚房	**mini-bar** 名 [ˋmɪnɪbɑr] （客房內的）冰箱酒櫃；迷你吧	**safe** 名 [sef] 保險箱

231

159

A Hello, Guest Services. This is Emily. How can I be of assistance?

您好，這裡是客務部的艾蜜莉，您需要什麼幫忙呢？

B I would like to order room service.

我想要叫客房服務。

🔊 Can I order room service now?

現在可以叫客房服務嗎？

A Sir, what is your room number and name, please?

先生，請問您的房號和大名？

B It's room 218 and the name is Smith.

我在 218 號房，名字是史密斯。

A What would you like to order?

您想要點什麼呢？

B I'd like the rump steak.

我要一份臀肉牛排。

A Would you like mashed potatoes, vegetables, or fries?

您要配馬鈴薯泥、蔬菜或是薯條嗎？

B Mashed potatoes and fries. Thank you.

我要馬鈴薯泥和薯條，謝謝。

A Which sauce would you prefer? We have pepper and mushroom.

您要加什麼醬料？我們有黑胡椒醬和蘑菇醬。

B I'll have mushroom sauce.

我要蘑菇醬。

A Is there anything else you'd like, sir?
先生，您還要點其他東西嗎？

B I'd also like the garden salad and a Coke.
我想要再加點一份田園沙拉和可樂。

Your order will be delivered to your room shortly.
Enjoy your meal.
我們將盡快將您的餐點送過去，祝您用餐愉快。

Thank you very much for your order. Please give us
a moment and I will be there with your order.
感謝您的點餐，請給我們一些時間準備餐點，我稍後將會把餐點送
過去您的房間。

Good morning, madam. This is your order.
早安，女士。您的餐點到了。

A What time would you like your wake-up call?
我們哪個時間叫您起床呢？

B I need two calls, one at 7 and another at 7:30.
我需要兩通電話，一通七點打，七點半再打另外一通。

A Actually, can I change the latter wake-up call to 8
a.m.?
可以把第二通電話改成早上八點嗎？

B I can certainly do that.
當然可以。

A I need one more towel and some soap.
我需要多一條毛巾和一些香皂。

B A maid will send them up in a minute.
服務人員稍後會幫您送過去。

一定用得到～
3句話搞定旅遊大小事

160

問有無某服務

Is a trainer available in the gym?
健身房裡面有教練嗎？

 也能這樣說：

Do you offer trainer services along with the gym?
健身房裡面有教練嗎？

對方可能這樣回應

> **I'm sorry, sir, but we have no trainers.**
> 很抱歉，先生，我們這邊沒有教練。

詢問使用方法

How can I use the personal safe in the closet?
衣櫃裡的保險箱怎麼用？

 也能這樣說：

Could you tell me how to use the personal safe in the closet?
可以教我怎麼用衣櫃裡的保險箱嗎？

對方可能這樣回應

> **Please follow the instructions on the safe.**
> 請照保險箱上面的指示操作就可以了。

可否代
訂票券

Can I book a city tour here?
我可以在這裡報名參加市區觀光嗎？

也能這樣說：

Are there any tour services at this hotel?
你們旅館有提供觀光的行程嗎？

對方可能這樣回應

The concierge can arrange it for you.
飯店服務台人員可以幫您預定行程。

旅途中也要會的單字　161

 娛樂設施

banquet 名 [`bæŋkwɪt] 宴會	**barbecue** 名 [`barbɪkju] 烤肉	**playground** 名 [`ple͵graʊnd] 遊樂場
sauna 名 [`saʊnə] 三溫暖	**spa** 名 [spa] 水療	**steam bath** 片 蒸汽浴
swimming pool 片 游泳池	**tennis court** 片 網球場	**Wi-Fi** 縮 無線網路

 豪華附加

24-7 片 全年無休	**barbershop** 名 [`barbə͵ʃap] 理髮店	**beauty shop** 片 美容院
chauffeur 名 [`ʃofə] 汽車司機	**luxurious** 形 [lʌg`ʒʊrɪəs] 豪華的；奢侈的	**massage** 名 [mə`saʒ] 按摩
secretarial service 片 祕書服務	**solarium** 名 [so`lɛrɪəm] 日光浴室	**state-of-the-art** 形 [`stetəvðɪ`art] 最先進的

162

A Can I leave the room key at the counter when I go out?

我外出時可以把鑰匙留在櫃檯嗎？

B We can certainly keep the key so you won't lose it.

我們可以幫您保留鑰匙，這樣您就不用怕遺失鑰匙了。

If you don't want to be disturbed, just hang the "Do not disturb" sign on your door knob.

如果你不想被打擾，把「請勿打擾」的牌子掛在門把上就可以了。

A Excuse me. Where can I send out some faxes and go on the Internet?

請問哪裡可以發傳真和上網？

B You can access the Internet and send faxes in our business center.

您可以到我們的商務中心發傳真和上網。

You can use your laptop to access the Internet in your room.

你可以用筆電連接房間裡面的網路線。

A What facilities are provided in the hotel?

你們飯店還有提供什麼設施呢？

B We have a gym, a sauna, and an indoor swimming pool.

我們有健身房、三溫暖，還有室內游泳池。

A How late is the sauna open?

三溫暖開到多晚呢？

B It's open 24 hours.

236

二十四小時都有開。

🔊 **We also have laundry services. You just need to leave your clothes in the laundry bag.**
我們還有提供洗衣服務，您只要把衣服放在洗衣袋裡面就可以了。

Ⓐ **Do you have a place where I can exercise?**
你們有什麼地方可以運動嗎？

Ⓑ **Yes, sir. We have a fine exercise facility.**
有的，先生，我們的運動中心很完善。

Ⓐ **Am I going to be charged extra for using the gym?**
使用健身房要收費嗎？

Ⓑ **You can use the gym for free. All you need is your room key.**
您可以免費使用健身房，只需要帶您的房卡就好了。

Ⓐ **What are the gym hours?**
健身房的開放時間是哪時候？

Ⓑ **Our gym is open around the clock, every day of the week.**
我們的健身房每天二十四小時都會開放。

Ⓐ **When do you serve breakfast?**
你們什麼時候提供早餐呢？

Ⓑ **From six to ten in the morning.**
上午六點到十點。

🔊 **Could you have these dry-cleaned, please?**
可以幫我把這些衣服送乾洗嗎？

Problems To Be Solved

解決住宿問題

一定用得到～
3句話搞定旅遊大小事

敘述
問題

The air conditioner is not working.
空調壞掉了。

🔊 也能這樣說：

The air conditioner seems to be broken.
空調好像壞了。

We'll send someone up in a minute to have a look.
我們等等會請人上去查看。

對方可能這樣回應

請人過
來修理

Could you send someone to fix it, please?
你可以派人過來修理一下嗎？

🔊 也能這樣說：

Could you please get it fixed as soon as possible?
可以盡快修理好這個問題嗎？

Sure, I'll send a plumber to fix it right away.
當然，我會立刻派水管工人去修理。

對方可能這樣回應

要求更
換房間

Can I change to another room?
我可以換房間嗎？

也能這樣說：

Could you arrange another room for me?
可以幫我換到其他房間嗎？

對方可能這樣回應

We'll give you a new room immediately.
我們會馬上幫您安排新的房間。

 旅途中也要會的單字 164

常見問題

bedding 名 [`bɛdɪŋ] 寢具	**cigarette** 名 [ˌsɪgəˋrɛt] 香菸	**cockroach** 名 [`kɑkˌrotʃ] 蟑螂
clog 動 [klɑg] 堵塞；塞滿	**dated** 形 [`detɪd] 陳舊的	**messy** 形 [`mɛsɪ] 雜亂的
odor 名 [`odə] 氣味	**rude** 形 [rud] 粗魯的	**theft** 名 [θɛft] 偷竊

其他問題

broken 形 [`brokən] 損壞的；被打破的	**dripping** 形 [`drɪpɪŋ] 滴水的	**leak** 名 [lik] 漏水
malfunction 名 [mælˋfʌŋkʃən] 故障	**noisy** 形 [`nɔɪzɪ] 吵鬧的	**pricey** 形 [`praɪsɪ] 高價的
smelly 形 [`smɛlɪ] 發臭的	**uncomfortable** 形 [ʌnˋkʌmfətəbḷ] 不舒服的	**unpleasant** 形 [ʌnˋplɛzn̩t] 令人不快的

The room smells like cigarette smoke.
這房間聞起來都是煙味。

- -

Do you want to change to another room?
你想要換成別的房間嗎？

- -

I can't believe that there isn't any hot water!
真不敢相信，這裡竟然沒有熱水！

- -

Ⓐ **Hello? This is room 1815. The shower doesn't work.**
喂？這裡是 1815 房，浴室水龍頭都沒有水。

Ⓑ **Someone will be there to fix it in a moment.**
我們馬上派人過去修。

- -

The toilet is clogged/stopped up.
馬桶塞住了。

- -

The sink isn't draining properly.
洗手台的水不通。

- -

You can use the house phone to call housekeeping.
你可以用內線電話打給客務部。

- -

May I have my bed sheet changed?
可以幫我換床單嗎？

- -

There are not enough towels in my room. Could you send more towels to my room?
我房間的毛巾不夠，麻煩再送幾條毛巾過來，謝謝。

A I have a little problem with room 816.
816 房有一些小問題。

B What exactly seems to be the problem, ma'am?
女士，您可以說一下有哪些問題嗎？

A I want a new room, and I want a refund for tonight.
我想要換房間，而且今晚的錢也應該退還給我。

B Would you please tell me the exact problem, sir?
先生，請問您想換房及退款的原因是什麼呢？

A Would you tell me the nature of the problem, sir?
先生，您有哪些問題呢？

B There are cockroaches crawling in my room.
我房間有一堆蟑螂。

A I specifically requested an ocean view, but the room I was given only has a view of the pool.
我有特別要求要海景房，但這個房間只看得到游泳池。

B I'm sorry about the mix up. We'll change your room immediately.
很抱歉將您的房間弄錯了，我會馬上幫您安排您要求的房間。

I'll find you another room immediately.
我馬上幫您安排另外一間房間。

A Couldn't we have another room?
我們不能換到別的房間嗎？

B I am very sorry, but all our rooms are occupied.
很抱歉，我們的房間全部都客滿了。

Unit
07
Checking Out & Settling The Bill

退房及結帳時

一定用得到～
3句話搞定旅遊大小事

麻煩客放行李
May I put my luggage here?
可以把行李寄放在這裡嗎？

 也能這樣說：

Could you keep my luggage until 3 p.m.?
你可以幫我保管行李到下午三點嗎？

> **Sure. You can leave your baggage here.**
> 沒問題，您可以將行李留在這裡。

對方可能這樣回答

要求延遲退房
Could I arrange for a late check-out?
我可以晚一點再退房嗎？

 也能這樣說：

Would it be possible to leave my room after the check-out time?
可以在規定的退房時間之後再退房嗎？

> **We can postpone your check-out time to 3 p.m. Will that be okay?**
> 我們可以把您的退房時間延到下午三點，這樣可以嗎？

對方可能這樣回答

242

帳單多收費用

There are some extra charges on my bill.
我的帳單上面有多的收費。

也能這樣說：

There seems to be a problem with my bill.
我的帳單好像有點問題。

Please wait a moment. I'll check it for you.
請稍等，我幫您查一下。

旅途中也要會的單字 167

退房注意

arrange 動 [ə`rendʒ] 整理；布置	**dispute** 動 [dɪ`spjut] 爭論	**key card** 片 電子房卡
late charge 片 延遲退房費用	**owe** 動 [o] 欠（錢等）	**procedure** 名 [prə`sidʒɚ] 手續
scrutinize 動 [`skrutn͵naɪz] 檢查	**settle up** 片 付清帳目	**storage** 名 [`storɪdʒ] 保管

住宿感想

acceptable 形 [ə`sɛptəbḷ] 可接受的	**affordable** 形 [ə`fɔrdəbḷ] 負擔得起的	**disappoint** 動 [͵dɪsə`pɔɪnt] 使失望
guest book 片 來賓留言簿	**meet sb.'s expectation** 片 符合某人的期望	**review** 名 動 [rɪ`vju] 評論
satisfactory 形 [͵sætɪs`fæktərɪ] 令人滿意的	**satisfy** 動 [`sætɪs͵faɪ] 使滿意	**worthy** 形 [`wɜðɪ] 值得的

What is your check-out time?
你們的退房時間是幾點？

I'll be checking out today.
我今天要退房。

I'd like to check out, please. This is my key.
我想要退房，這是我的鑰匙。

Is there an extra charge for the late check-out?
延遲退房會多收費嗎？

Could you please have my bill ready?
可以先幫我把帳單準備好嗎？

A Did you take anything from the mini-bar today?
您今天有拿迷你吧裡面的東西嗎？

B Yes, we had two bottles of apple juice.
有，我們喝了兩瓶蘋果汁。

I didn't make any long-distance phone calls.
我沒有從房間打任何長途電話。

We didn't drink anything from the mini-bar except for mineral water.
我們除了礦泉水以外，沒有再從迷你吧裡面拿其他飲料。

Aren't the snacks in the room free?
房間裡面的點心不是免費的嗎？

244

Ⓐ **You also charged me for a movie, but I didn't order any movies.**
你們還扣了電影的費用，但我沒有看電影。

Ⓑ **I am sorry. We have given you the wrong bill.**
很抱歉，我們給錯帳單了。

Why am I being charged $10 for a movie that I never ordered?
為什麼我被收了十元的電影費？我沒有看任何電影啊。

Ⓐ **How would you like to pay?**
請問您要怎麼付款？

Ⓑ **I'd like to pay by credit card, please.**
我要用信用卡。

Please sign on the dotted line.
請在虛線上簽名。

Thank you, Mr. Lin. Your credit card deposit will be refunded to you shortly.
林先生，謝謝您，押金將會退還到您的信用卡。

Ⓐ **Do you want me to call a taxi for you?**
需要我幫您叫計程車嗎？

Ⓑ **No, thanks. I am taking the airport shuttle.**
不用了，謝謝。我要搭機場接駁車。

Thank you for staying. We hope to serve you again in the near future.
謝謝您住宿本飯店，希望很快就有機會能再為您服務。

Thank you. And here's your receipt, sir.
謝謝，先生，這裡是您的收據。

Part 7

解決突發狀況

Resolving Problems

How to deal with problems during your journey?

不怕一萬，只怕萬一，遇到緊急事件這樣做就對了！

名 名詞　　動 動詞　　形 形容詞

副 副詞　　介 介係詞　　片 片語　　縮 縮寫

01 Reporting A Theft To The Police
被偷被搶怎麼辦

一定用得到～
3句話搞定旅遊大小事

請人阻止小偷

Thief! Stop him!
有小偷！阻止那個人！

也能這樣說：

Catch that man in black!
抓住那個穿黑衣的男人！

Stop that man! Somebody call the police!
阻止那個人！誰去報警一下！

警方可能這樣回應

走進警局報案

I want to report a theft.
我想要申報一件竊盜案。

也能這樣說：

I'd like to file a report for stolen property.
我想要報案，我的東西被偷了。

OK. I need you to fill out the form first.
好的，請你先填這張表格。

警方可能這樣回應

說明被偷遭遇

I was robbed!
我被搶了！

也能這樣說：

I was mugged by a young man in black.
我被一個身穿黑衣的年輕人搶了。

Did you get a good look at the person who robbed you?
你有看清楚搶你的人長什麼樣子嗎？

 對方可能這樣回答

 旅途中也要會的單字 170

 遭遇竊盜

burglar 名 [`bɝglɚ] 竊賊	**mug** 動 [mʌg] 搶劫	**pickpocket** 名 [`pɪk.pakɪt] 扒手
rob 動 [rab] 搶劫	**robbery** 名 [`rabərɪ] 搶劫案	**shoplift** 動 [`ʃap.lɪft] 冒充顧客在商店行竊
snatch 名 動 [snætʃ] 搶奪	**steal** 動 [stil] 偷竊	**thief** 名 [θif] 小偷

警察局報案

cop 名 [kap] 警察	**detective** 名 [dɪ`tɛktɪv] 刑警；偵探	**marshal** 名 [`marʃəl] （美）警察局長
officer 名 [`ɔfəsɚ] 警官	**on duty** 片 值勤	**patrol** 名 動 [pə`trol] 巡邏
police force 片 警力	**police station** 片 警察局	**sheriff** [`ʃɛrɪf]（美）警長

171

🔊 Should I help you file a report with the police?
要不要我幫你向警方報案？

Ⓐ Where is the nearest police station?
離這裡最近的警察局在哪裡呢？

Ⓑ There is a police station around the corner.
轉角就有一間警察局。

Ⓐ What are the police going to ask?
警察會問我什麼呢？

Ⓑ They'll probably ask you to describe what happened.
他們可能會請你描述一下事情是怎麼發生的。

🔊 I had my pocket picked.
我被扒了。

🔊 Is it possible to find the pickpocket?
有沒有辦法找到扒手呢？

🔊 A man grabbed my purse in front of the train station and ran away.
有個人在火車站前搶了我的錢包就跑了。

Ⓐ What does the man look like?
他長什麼樣子？

Ⓑ I didn't see him clearly, but he wore a blue sweater.
我沒有看清楚他的臉，不過他穿藍色的毛衣。

🔊 He's around middle age, not tall.
他大概四、五十歲，長得不高。

Ⓐ When can I hear from you?
什麼時候會有消息？

Ⓑ We'll contact you as soon as we have further information.
如果有進一步的消息，我們會盡快通知您。

📢 Somebody stole my backpack.
有人偷了我的背包。

Ⓐ What color is your backpack?
你的背包是什麼顏色？

Ⓑ My backpack is dark blue.
我的背包是深藍色的。

Ⓐ What's inside your backpack?
你的背包裡面有什麼東西？

Ⓑ A brown wallet, a guide book, and a laptop.
有一個棕色皮夾、一本旅遊書和一台筆記型電腦。

📢 He was caught shoplifting.
他因為順手牽羊被捕。

Ⓐ Is anything missing?
有沒有東西不見了？

Ⓑ Everything is there, except for some cash.
除了一些現金之外，其他東西都在。

📢 Were there any witnesses?
有沒有目擊者？

📢 The thief was caught by the police.
警察抓到小偷了。

一定用得到～
3句話搞定旅遊大小事

172

問處理
程序

I lost my passport. What should I do?
我的護照掉了，應該怎麼辦才好？

也能這樣說：

Do you know how to report a missing passport?
你知道護照遺失應該要怎麼處理嗎？

對方可能這樣回應

You need to contact the embassy right away.
你必須馬上連絡大使館。

詢問補
發護照

Where can I get a new passport?
我要到哪裡辦新護照呢？

也能這樣說：

Where should I apply for reissue?
我要在哪裡申請補發護照呢？

對方可能這樣回應

You'd better go to the ROC Overseas Mission and get more details.
你最好到駐外處詢問細節。

掛失信用卡時

I'd like to report a missing credit card, please.
我要掛失信用卡，麻煩你了。

也能這樣說：

I am here to report the loss of my credit card.
我想要掛失我的信用卡。

May I have your name, please?
請問您的貴姓大名？

對方可能這樣回應

旅途中也要會的單字 173

重要物品

bank statement 片 銀行結單	**certificate** 名 [səˋtɪfəkɪt] 證明文件	**copy** 名 動 [ˋkɑpɪ] 拷貝
document 名 [ˋdɑkjəmənt] 文件	**ID card** 片 身分證	**passport photo** 片 護照用的相片
travel document 片 旅遊文件	**vaccination certificate** 片 疫苗接種證明	**valuable** 形 [ˋvæljuəbḷ] 貴重的

嘗試處理

customer service line 片 客服電話	**diplomat** 名 [ˋdɪpləmæt] 外交官	**embassy** 名 [ˋɛmbəsɪ] 大使館
emergency contact 片 緊急聯絡人	**issue** 動 [ˋɪʃju] 核發	**reissue** 動 [riˋɪʃju] 重新核發
ROC Overseas Mission 片 中華民國駐外處	**toll-free** 形 [ˏtolˋfri] 免費撥打的	**travel insurance** 片 旅遊保險

First, you should fill out a Report of Loss at a local police station.
你必須先到附近警局拿失竊證明。

Then, you should get a new passport as soon as possible.
然後，你最好盡快辦理新護照。

The embassy will be able to help you replace your passport.
大使館人員可以幫你換發新護照。

How long will it take to get my passport reissued?
補發護照要多久呢？

Ⓐ **Do you have a passport photo with you?**
您有護照用的照片嗎？

Ⓑ **Yes, I always prepare two passport photos in case of any problems.**
有，我都會準備兩張護照相片，如果有突發狀況就可以用到。

You have to fill out the form and pay the fee.
你必須填寫這張表格，並支付申請費。

Ⓐ **What else can I do?**
還有什麼我能做的嗎？

Ⓑ **Call the bank and cancel your credit cards.**
你必須打電話到銀行，中止你的信用卡。

You should also ask the bank to stop payment.

你也應該要求銀行止付所有費用。

A Hi, I'm calling to report a stolen credit card.
你好，我想要報失信用卡。

B May I have your name and ID number, please?
請給我您的姓名以及身分證字號。

You can cancel your card temporarily and wait to see if it turns up.
您可以先暫時停掉信用卡，然後看之後會不會找到。

You can also cancel it permanently, and we'll send you a new card.
您也可以選擇剪掉您的信用卡，這樣我們會寄新卡給您。

My traveler's checks have been stolen.
我的旅行支票被偷了。

May I see your receipts?
我可以看一下您的存根聯嗎？

I didn't sign those lost traveler's checks.
我沒有在遺失的旅支上面簽名。

We don't replace any unsigned checks.
我們不補發沒有簽名的支票。

You should have signed them first when you bought them.
買旅行支票時，你就應該要先在上面簽名。

一定用得到～
3句話搞定旅遊大小事

175

詢問失物招領
I am looking for the lost-and-found counter.
我在找失物招領櫃檯。

也能這樣說：

Where should I claim my lost items?
我要到哪裡領回遺失的東西呢？

The lost-and-found counter is on the first floor.
失物招領櫃檯在一樓。

對方可能這樣回應

遺失時的地點
I left my cell phone on the bus.
我的手機掉在公車上面了。

也能這樣說：

My cell phone went missing as I went off the bus.
我下公車時，手機就不見了。

You can phone the bus company and see if they picked up any lost phones on the bus.
你可以打給客運公司，看看他們有沒有在公車上撿到手機。

對方可能這樣回應

描述遺失物品

It's a blue canvas backpack.
我的背包是藍色的帆布背包。

 也能這樣說：

My backpack is blue, and it's made of canvas.
我的背包是藍色的、帆布做的。

And what's in your bag?
那你的包包裡面有什麼東西？

 對方可能這樣回應

 ✈ **旅途中也要會的單字** 176

🔖 遺落物品

backpack 名 [`bæk͵pæk] 背包	**belonging** 名 [bɪ`lɔŋɪŋ] 所有物	**duffel bag** 片 （圓筒狀的）行李袋
folding umbrella 片 摺疊雨傘	**handbag** 名 [`hænd͵bæg] 手提袋	**key** 名 [ki] 鑰匙
purse 名 [pɜs] （女用）錢包	**tablet PC** 片 平板電腦	**wallet** 名 [`wɑlɪt] 皮夾

🔖 失物招領

forget 動 [fɚ`gɛt] 忘記	**leave** 動 [liv] 遺忘	**leave sth. behind** 片 忘了帶某物；留下某物
look for sth. 片 尋找某物	**lose** 動 [luz] 遺失	**lost and found** 片 失物招領處
search 動 [sɝtʃ] 尋找	**valuable** 名 [`væljuəbḷ] 貴重物品	**invaluable** 形 [ɪn`væljəbḷ] 非常貴重的

Ⓐ What's the matter?
發生什麼事了？

Ⓑ I've lost my handbag.
我的手提包不見了。

Ⓐ Where did you lose it?
你在哪裡掉的？

Ⓑ Well, I don't know exactly.
我不太確定耶。

I have no idea where I left it.
我完全不知道是在哪裡掉的。

You should have a look in the hotel room first.
你應該先回飯店房間找找看。

I left it in the restaurant, but I couldn't find it when I went back.
我把它忘在餐廳了，但我回去找就找不到了。

Ⓐ Are there any valuable things in your bag?
你的包包裡面有什麼貴重物品嗎？

Ⓑ Yes. I put everything in it. My wallet, passport, camera, and cell phone.
有，我的東西全部都在裡面，有皮夾、護照、相機和手機。

Ⓐ What was in your wallet?
你的皮夾裡面有什麼呢？

Ⓑ My credit cards and 300 U.S. dollars in cash.

裡面有我的信用卡，還有三百塊美金。

A I left my camera in the cab.
我把相機忘在計程車裡面了。

B Do you remember the plate number?
你還記得車號嗎？

Please give me your name, address, and telephone number.
請告訴我您的名字、住址和聯絡電話。

We'll call you if your camera is found.
如果有找到您的相機，我們就會打給您。

A Have you seen a black leather wallet?
請問你們有撿到一個黑色的皮夾嗎？

B Is this your wallet?
這個是你的皮夾嗎？

Has anyone picked up a camera on the bus?
有人在公車上撿到我的相機嗎？

A I dropped my umbrella on the train.
我的雨傘掉在火車上。

B No one has picked up any umbrella today, but you can file a report here.
今天還沒有人撿到雨傘，不過你可以先在這裡報失你的物品。

Please fill in this form first, and you can have your wallet back.
請先填寫這張表格，填完你就可以把皮夾拿回去了。

一定用得到～
3句話搞定旅遊大小事

178

描述
喉嚨痛

I have a sore throat.
我喉嚨很痛。

也能這樣說：

My throat feels raw/sore.
我喉嚨很痛。

對方可能這樣回應

Do you cough a lot these days?
你最近會一直咳嗽嗎？

胃痛
的時候

I have a stomachache.
我胃痛。

也能這樣說：

My stomach aches really bad.
我的胃很痛。

對方可能這樣回應

Does it hurt all the time?
是一直都感覺很痛嗎？

260

需要急救箱時

Do you have a first-aid kit with you right now?
你現在身上有急救箱嗎？

也能這樣說：

Do you happen to have a first-aid kit handy?
你手邊剛好有急救箱嗎？

對方可能這樣回答

Here. I have some band-aids and alcohol.
我有一些 OK 繃和酒精，給你吧。

旅途中也要會的單字　179

 各種症狀

bleed 動 [blid] 流血	**catch a cold** 片 感冒	**cough** 名 動 [kɔf] 咳嗽
headache 名 [`hɛd͵ek] 頭痛	**injury** 名 [`ɪndʒərɪ] 受傷	**sneeze** 動 [sniz] 打噴嚏
sore throat 片 喉嚨痛	**stomachache** 名 [`stʌmək͵ek] 胃痛；腹痛	**wound** 名 [wund] 傷口

 身體不適

ache 名 動 [ek] 疼痛	**bandage** 名 [`bændɪdʒ] 繃帶	**dizzy** 形 [`dɪzɪ] 頭暈目眩的
hurt 動 [hɜt] 疼痛；使受傷	**over-the-counter** 形 [`ovəðə`kaʊntə] 不用處方簽的	**pain** 名 [pen] 疼痛
pale 形 [pel] 蒼白的	**prescription** 名 [prɪ`skrɪpʃən] 藥方	**under the weather** 片 身體不舒服

A I am not feeling well.
我的身體不太舒服。

B You'd better go see a doctor.
你最好還是去看醫生吧。

Is there a clinic nearby?
這附近有診所嗎？

A Are you all right? You look pale.
你還好吧？你看起來很蒼白耶。

B I think I am about to catch a cold.
我覺得我快要感冒了。

I have phlegm in my throat and have difficulty breathing.
我喉嚨裡面有痰，讓我覺得很難呼吸。

How long have you been feeling dizzy?
你從什麼時候開始感覺頭很暈呢？

A What symptoms do you have?
你有什麼症狀呢？

B I have an upset stomach.
我有點反胃。

When did this start?
什麼時候開始有這個症狀的呢？

Where exactly does it hurt?
哪個部位會痛？

Does it hurt when I press here?
按這裡會痛嗎？

Ⓐ **Did you vomit?**
你有吐嗎？

Ⓑ **I have vomited and have watery diarrhea.**
我有吐，而且還拉肚子。

You are bleeding! Let me get you some bandages.
你在流血耶！我幫你拿一些繃帶吧。

Ⓐ **What's happened? The cut looks serious.**
怎麼了？傷口看起來怎麼那麼深。

Ⓑ **I cut myself accidently.**
我不小心割到自己了。

I have a sore throat. Which medicine should I take?
喉嚨痛要吃哪種藥？

Do you have aspirin?
你們有賣阿斯匹靈嗎？

Is this medicine for muscle aches?
這種藥可以減緩肌肉痠痛嗎？

What pills should I take for my flu symptoms?
有感冒症狀的話，要吃哪種藥才好？

What are the side effects of this medicine?
這種藥的副作用有哪些呢？

一定用得到～
3句話搞定旅遊大小事

181

請人叫
救護車

Call an ambulance!
快叫救護車！

🔊 也能這樣說：

Call 911 ！
快打 119 ！

對方可能這樣回應

OK. Help is on the way.
打好了，救護車要來了。

車禍事
故報案

I need to report an accident.
我想要報案，這裡有一起車禍。

🔊 也能這樣說：

Two cars collided head-on here on 5th Avenue.
在第五大道有兩部車正面相撞。

對方可能這樣回應

Is anyone hurt?
有人受傷嗎？

264

He has a serious head injury.
他頭部外傷很嚴重。

也能這樣說：

He has a critical head injury.
他頭部受了重傷。

Is the victim conscious?
病患還有意識嗎？

旅途中也要會的單字 182

 緊急事故

accident 名 [`æksədənt] 意外；事故	**ambulance** 名 [`æmbjələns] 救護車	**blood pressure** 片 血壓
car accident 片 車禍	**conscious** 形 [`kɑnʃəs] 有意識的	**hit-and-run** 形 [`hɪtn̩`rʌn] 肇事逃逸的
hospitalization 名 [ˌhɑspɪtl̩ə`zeʃən] 住院	**paramedic** 名 [ˌpɛrə`mɛdɪk] 急救員	**stretcher** 名 [`strɛtʃɚ] 擔架

 急救術語

AED 縮 自動體外心臟電擊去顫器	**blood transfusion** 片 輸血	**CPR** 縮 心肺復甦術
emergency room (ER) 片 急診室	**golden hour** 片 黃金救援時間（一小時）	**Heimlich maneuver** 片 哈姆立克急救法
intensive care unit (ICU) 片 加護病房	**nursing station** 片 護理站	**operating room (OR)** 片 手術室

A 911. What's your emergency?
這裡是 119，有什麼需要幫忙的？

B There's an overturned truck on Highway 37.
37 號高速公路有台翻覆的大卡車。

There was a chain-reaction accident on the highway.
高速公路上有一起連環車禍。

One car turned upside-down, and several cars were badly damaged in the collision.
有一輛車翻覆了，然後好幾部車追撞，都嚴重變形。

We have no idea how the accident happened.
我們完全不知道這個事故是怎麼發生的。

A distracted driver caused the serious accident.
這個心不在焉的駕駛造成這場嚴重的意外。

The little girl was a witness to the car crash.
那個小女孩是這場車禍的目擊證人。

There are five dead and three injured in the traffic accident.
這場車禍造成五死三傷。

One of the victims passed out. Call an ambulance!
有一位受害者昏倒了，快叫救護車！

He needs first aid!
他需要急救！

All the injured people were taken to the local hospital.
所有的傷患都被送到當地的醫院了。

The boy needs a blood transfusion.
這個小男孩需要輸血。

A Is he conscious?
他還有意識嗎？

B Yes, he is conscious.
有，他意識還很清楚。

Don't worry! It's just a slight injury, not a major one.
別擔心！這只是輕傷，不是重傷。

A 12-year-old boy is the only survivor.
這位十二歲的男童是唯一的生還者。

We're done. You may go home and rest now.
我們處理完傷口了，你可以回家休息了。

Please come back to have your stitches removed next week.
下週請回門診拆線。

I had a six-stitch suture on my arm last Sunday.
我上星期日手臂縫了六針。

What's wrong? How did you hurt yourself?
怎麼了？你怎麼受傷了？

Travel NOTE

國家圖書館出版品預行編目資料

想去哪就去哪！用3句英文去旅行 / 張翔 編著. -- 初版
. -- 新北市：知識工場出版 采舍國際有限公司發行，
2017.12　面；　公分. --（速充Focus；01）
ISBN 978-986-271-793-6（平裝）

1.英語　2.旅遊　3.會話

805.188　　　　　　　　　　106017440

▌知識工場 · 速充Focus 01

想去哪就去哪！
用3句英文去旅行

出 版 者／全球華文聯合出版平台·知識工場
作　　者／張翔　　　　　　　　印 行 者／知識工場
出版總監／王寶玲　　　　　　　英文編輯／何毓翔
總 編 輯／歐綾纖　　　　　　　美術設計／蔡億盈

郵撥帳號／50017206 采舍國際有限公司（郵撥購買，請另付一成郵資）
台灣出版中心／新北市中和區中山路2段366巷10號10樓
電話／（02）2248-7896
傳真／（02）2248-7758
ISBN-13／978-986-271-793-6
出版日期／2017年12月初版

全球華文市場總代理／采舍國際
地址／新北市中和區中山路2段366巷10號3樓
電話／（02）8245-8786
傳真／（02）8245-8718

港澳地區總經銷／和平圖書
地址／香港柴灣嘉業街12號百樂門大廈17樓
電話／（852）2804-6687
傳真／（852）2804-6409

全系列書系特約展示
新絲路網路書店
地址／新北市中和區中山路2段366巷10號10樓
電話／（02）8245-9896
傳真／（02）8245-8819
網址／www.silkbook.com

本書採減碳印製流程並使用優質中性紙（Acid & Alkali Free）通過綠色印刷認證，最符環保要求。

本書為名師張翔及出版社編輯小組精心編著覆核，如仍有疏漏，請各位先進不吝指正。來函請寄 ginho@mail.book4u.com.tw，若經查證無誤，我們將有精美小禮物贈送！